FIRE

Although not originally intent on becoming a children's author, Geoffrey Trease, born in 1909, has always loved writing and history, and was able to combine the two in his first children's novel – *Bows Against the Barons*, published in 1934. Since then he has written some eighty books for children and a number of adults' works, including novels and a history of London. His works have appeared in twenty-six countries and twenty languages. Many have been dramatized as radio serials in the BBC's *Children's Hour*.

Geoffrey Trease has travelled widely in Europe, lived in Russia and served in India in the Second World War. He now lives in Bath, next door to his daughter, Jocelyn. He also has four granddaughters, twin great-granddaughters and a great-grandson – but, as he says, "no other pets"!

*Fire on the Wind* is his 103rd book!

*Titles by Geoffrey Trease*

# Fire on the Wind

Geoffrey Trease

**PIPER**

PAN MACMILLAN

CHILDREN'S BOOKS

First published 1993 by Pan Macmillan Children's Books

This Piper edition published 1994 by Pan Macmillan Children's Books
a division of Pan Macmillan Publishers Limited
Cavaye Place London SW10 9PG
and Basingstoke

Associated companies throughout the world

ISBN 0 330 33362 3

1 3 5 7 9 8 6 4 2

A CIP catalogue record for this book is available from
the British Library

Phototypeset by Intype, London
Printed and bound in Great Britain by
Cox & Wyman Ltd, Reading, Berkshire

For
Margaret Meek

## AUTHOR'S NOTE

Few historical events are as well documented, with eye-witness accounts and contemporary records, as the Fire of London in 1666. This evidence is collected in Walter G. Bell's *The Great Fire of London*, first published in 1920. But, as we see in our own newspapers, honest witnesses can give contradictory evidence of the same event. There are several versions of when and why the episode at St Faith's came to end as it most certainly did. In such cases a fiction writer can only choose one version and stick to it, as I have done.

Bath, 1992
G. T.

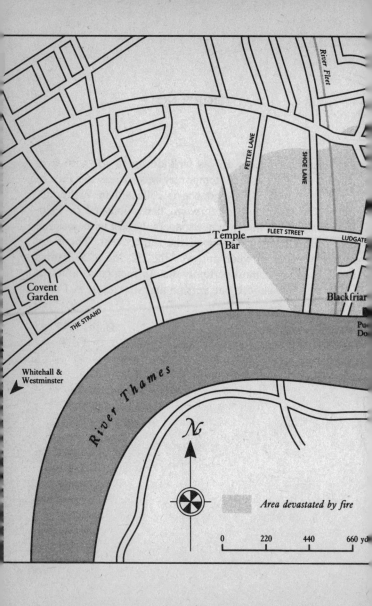

River Fleet

FETTER LANE

SHOE LANE

Temple Bar

FLEET STREET

LUDGATE

Covent Garden

Blackfriar

THE STRAND

Pu
Do

Whitehall & Westminster

River Thames

N

Area devastated by fire

0    220    440    660 yd

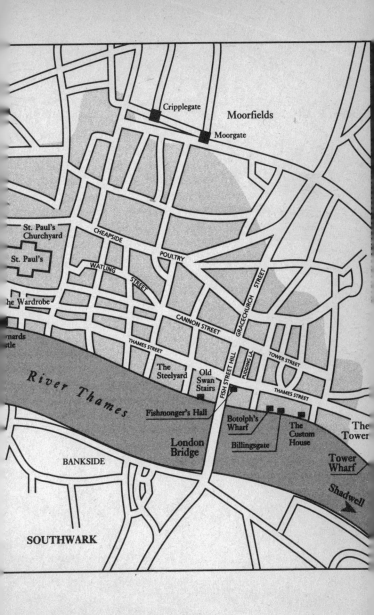

# 1

At their first meeting Sarah and Hugh got off on the wrong foot.

Hugh was already in a black mood. Mr Biddulph, waking with a thick head after last night at the tavern, had humiliated him in front of the older servants and then sent him on a needless errand across the city.

Hugh was consoling himself in the only way he could. On many of these errands he could include a detour through St Paul's Churchyard, a livelier place than one might expect from its name.

The graves had been levelled ages ago, the dead forgotten. The space round the dilapidated cathedral had been paved over, all of twelve acres Hugh reckoned with his countryman's eye. That area was hemmed in by surviving church buildings, St Paul's School and the High Master's house, and by shops and taverns, like Sampson's or the Golden Anchor, that had sprung up in recent years. Other traders spread out their stock on open stalls. It was more like the markets he remembered from his native Herefordshire.

Only – and this specially attracted him – it had booksellers. It was known for them. There were over twenty, and customers moved from one to another in quest of the latest book or broadsheet, or of some rare volume now long out of print. Hugh loved to get among them. He might not have a penny in his pocket but there was pleasure in the mere sight and smell of print, the feel of a fine binding under

1

his fingertips. For a brief moment he could escape into the memory of happier days.

Today a pamphlet caught his eye. *How to Get Rich*, by someone named Hugh Audley – his own first name – was that an omen? He had started with "only" two hundred pounds and died worth four hundred thousand. But the pamphlet proved dull, all about keeping accounts of income and expenses, with cheerless do's and don'ts such as "Drink not the third glass." This worthy but unnecessary advice was interrupted by a sharp cry of "*Boy!*"

Hugh flinched. It was almost the tone Mr Biddulph would have used. But it was not his voice, it was a girl's. Glancing across the book-strewn stall he saw the fair-haired girl he had often noticed – what boy wouldn't? – but had never spoken to. She was no older than himself. His temper flashed.

"Were you speaking to *me*?"

She turned and stared, open-mouthed. The colour rushed into her face. "*You?*" She laughed, embarrassed. "Of course not! You must forgive me—" She called again, in the same imperious tone: "Boy!"

There was a soft scuttling and out from a forest of human legs shot a small dog, black and grey and white, with absurdly floppy ears. She stooped to fondle him. "What a *bad* Boy! Going off like that!" She faced Hugh again. "He's supposed to help me mind the stall. Lie down!" The spaniel stretched himself obediently beneath the trestle table. "I named him," she explained, "after the famous one."

"The famous one?"

"You know – Prince Rupert's. In the great rebellion. Only *he* was white. But you're just as beautiful," she hastily assured the dog. "He slept in the Prince's bed when they were on campaign. He charged with the Cavaliers at Marston Moor – the Prince found his body afterwards, where the thick of the fighting had been."

2

"I'm sorry. I didn't know."

"I thought everybody knew about the Prince's Boy."

He was vexed with himself for not knowing. He said: "And yours helps you mind the stall?"

"Yes – for my grandfather, Mr Calamy. If there's anything you want – I know the stock." She sounded, he thought, remarkably confident. He was surprised, and was clumsy in hiding the fact.

"Isn't that unusual? I mean—"

"For a mere female?" There was quiet danger now in her voice.

"Well . . ." He was floundering. "In the ordinary way—"

"We *can* read and write, you know. But, if there's nothing you wish to buy—"

She knows perfectly well, he thought bitterly, that I've no money for books. "Not today," he said. "I'm just looking. That is, if you don't mind?"

"You're welcome. Though" – she had not missed the sarcasm in his voice, and mischievously echoed his earlier words – "isn't it a little unusual?"

"For a boy like me?"

"Well . . ." She hesitated. Her smile was almost a grin. "Most of our customers are old clergymen or—"

He wanted to cry out, Not grubby footboys! And tell her that only bad luck had doomed him to run errands for a fishmonger. He wanted to explain that he had been an apprentice to a printer, that he understood about type and paper and binding, and that if things had gone differently—

But their conversation was cut short by a customer, not an old clergyman but a swaggering gentleman, who spoke like a foreigner.

"I look everywhere, Mademoiselle, for a dictionary!"

"For the French language, sir?"

"For the English. I, naturally, am French."

"The best dictionary is Randle Cotgrave's—"

3

"That was the name!"

"Published in 1611, reprinted – much enlarged – in 1660."

"Ah! You have this book?"

"I – I am not certain. If you could come back, sir, in a little while, perhaps my grandfather—"

So, thought Hugh with satisfaction, there were limits to her knowledge.

"I will make a promenade in the church, Mademoiselle. In half an hour, then?"

The gentleman strolled away towards the cathedral porch. The interior served nowadays as a general rendezvous, a place to meet friends or clients, or, as Hugh had done in his time, study notices of vacant jobs, or treat as a general gossip-shop.

The girl turned back to Hugh. "You look honest," she said swiftly.

"Thank you!"

"Would you watch the stall for a few minutes? If any one asks for my grandfather – Mr Calamy – could you explain—"

"I think I'm equal to that."

She sped away and was lost in the crowd. He knew he could spare another quarter of an hour, or even longer. No one was waiting impatiently for his return. The household was overstaffed. Mr Biddulph kept servants for show. He was not content to be just a prominent figure in the Company of Fishmongers, he longed to become an alderman, perhaps even one day Lord Mayor.

The time passed quickly. The table was heaped with alluring volumes. Plays – when, he wondered, would the theatres reopen, now that the plague was over that had closed them last year? *Hamlet* . . . He was far away in fancy on the ghostly battlements of Elsinore when suddenly the girl was at his side, breathless and pink with triumph. She was holding a book, Cotgrave's French and English dictionary.

4

"I knew I had seen a copy at Mr Fletcher's!" Her tone changed as she stared into the distance. "Oh. My grandfather is coming back."

"So now your worries are over." But she had not sounded particularly pleased. Then, with relief in her voice, she said:

"Ah, he's met Dr Crumlum! He's a great talker. And no one interrupts Dr Crumlum. He's High Master at the school."

Hugh followed her stare. Even without cap and gown Dr Crumlum was unmistakably a headmaster. He towered over the paunchy little bookseller. Authority exuded from him.

Meanwhile the Frenchman was returning. The girl welcomed him eagerly. Suddenly her grandfather had become unessential. Dr Crumlum could detain him indefinitely.

"I have found the dictionary, Monsieur. It's in excellent condition."

"I am vastly obliged. Do you know how much it is?"

She did not hesitate. "Eighteen shillings."

He pulled out a handful of coins and diffidently held out a golden guinea. "This is sufficient, yes?"

"More than sufficient, Monsieur." She handed him his change in shillings. Some people, thought Hugh, would have been tempted to cheat a foreigner.

The gentleman went off delighted. Mr Calamy, freed at last, came waddling back to his stall. "We owe Mr Fletcher twelve shillings," said the girl hurriedly. "Shall I run with it now?" Hugh caught only the end of her whispered explanation . . . "So I charged the Frenchman eighteen and he seemed well satisfied!"

"Good girl! You're learning, Sarah. No lad could do better." The girl laughed and hurried away. Hugh moved off towards Fish Street Hill. There was nothing to stay for.

# 2

Would she see him again today, Sarah wondered as she swung her legs out of bed and crossed barefoot to the little window. It faced east to the looming mass of Baynards Castle. She could smell the salty freshness as the tide came swirling into Puddle Dock. Gulls wheeled over the steep gables.

Another fine day. No rain now for weeks. Washing her face, she thought how lucky they were to have clean water piped straight into their kitchen. People with their own wells complained that the level was getting low. You could not trust the men who sold water in pails at the door. Most likely it was topped up from the filthy river.

It would be hot again in the churchyard. They would be thankful when the sun moved round and the cathedral cast a wing of shade over their stall.

She was getting used to her new life. One gets used to everything, she told herself, even the loss of one's mother. It had been easier with her father's death – that was three years ago, anyhow, and he had been away so much. A seaman's child was always braced against possible disaster. That her mother should die had been unthinkable, even during the pestilence, when people were dying like flies. Yet the unthinkable had happened. And in her mother's case it had not actually been the plague. That made no difference. Suddenly life had shattered like a dropped jug. She had moved in with her grandfather, there had been nowhere

6

else. She was still picking up pieces, dumbly trying to fit them together.

At least the new life had its distractions. The bustle of Paul's Churchyard, the pageant of passing humanity, the fascination of all those books . . . and the house Grandfather rented at Puddle Dock, the boats constantly coming in and out, the merchants and ship's captains and Whitehall notables they set ashore, the watermen themselves so jovial and lusty, so full of ale and song.

Now, as she combed her hair, her thoughts returned to the boy. She saw plenty of boys as she stood behind the stall, prentices of every trade, schoolboys arriving like snails and racing home like liberated monkeys . . . and their seniors who sometimes paused by the stall, less interested in books than in teasing her with their sly wit and double meanings. But she was learning fast to hold her own.

Yesterday's dark-haired youth had been somehow different. No schoolboy – but well schooled. He had picked up Ovid's poems. Under her eyelashes she had observed his lips moving silently. He knows Latin, she thought enviously. She was not sure whether she liked him or not. She was just curious. Would he pass through the churchyard today?

She left her tumbled bed to the maid. Fanny had her own work, as she had hers. It was a long day at the stall and Grandfather prided himself on being there as early as anyone. She hurried downstairs. The spaniel rushed in from the yard to greet her. Mary poured her a mug of milk, just delivered by the milkmaid. Even the cow lived in a shed in the next lane. Grandfather did not trouble with breakfast. He would take his morning draught later with his bookseller cronies in one of the taverns.

"But you're too young to give up breakfast, Miss Sarah," the cook reminded her firmly. "You're still growing."

7

"I know that," she said contentedly, and sank her teeth into a hunk of bread.

She had barely finished it when she heard her grandfather's uncertain tread upon the stairs. His sight troubled him nowadays. "A blind bookseller is a contradiction in terms," he would lament. Sarah thought it magical the way he could identify a favourite volume by the mere feel of its binding, calf or whatever, and the smell of its crackling pages as he held it up to his fading eyes.

"Not magic," he would say with a chuckle. "No more than when you young folk play blindman's buff. You can guess the girl you've caught – or the boy – never mind the blindfold!"

She laughed. But it was a long time, she thought sadly, since she had played.

He'd reached the foot of the stairs now. She saw, before he clapped on his hat, how his lank grey hair was thinning. She wished he would take to a wig like other gentlemen. He made the excuse that this was no time to buy one. It was rumoured that new wigs were being made from the hair of plague victims. She shuddered and did not suggest it again.

The plague had almost worn itself out in London, though it lingered in smaller towns. The bishops would set no date for a public thanksgiving and the theatres remained shut. The shadow still hung over the city.

They stepped out into the sunshine, Boy frisking at their heels. Blackfriars was an odd little quarter, site of a religious foundation closed down by Henry the Eighth. Great noblemen had built mansions here and made the area fashionable. Those days were past, the mansions had been divided into tenements, though the King's Great Wardrobe was still there, a big building close by Puddle Dock, housing the royal robes and liveries. Smaller dwellings had been squeezed in, like Mr Calamy's. With the Thames to the south, and its tributary, the Fleet, blocking any expansion westwards, the area was now overcrowded and run down. But it suited Jonathan Calamy, being so handy for Paul's Churchyard, and Sarah was learning to love it.

The bigger booksellers had houses actually fronting on the churchyard, hanging out their signs, such as the White Greyhound, and using an outhouse as a printshop if they held the Archbishop of Canterbury's licence to publish their own books. That was restricted to only twenty-two members of the Stationers Company.

Sarah's grandfather had no such ambitions. At night he left his stock in a shed rented from one of the taverns. The stock was not vast. He was selective, he knew his regular customers and what he could sell. She would tease him, saying, "You're not really a bookseller – you're a book-*lover*." His turnover was just enough to live on. Until his sight worsened he had always been happy to sit reading. Nowadays, with Sarah to mind the stall, he spent more time gossiping over a glass of wine with his friends.

She, for her part, never minded being left with only her dog for company, dipping into one book after another, having a word with a neighbouring stallholder, studying the ever-changing crowd, identifying well-known individuals.

That morning, even before her grandfather departed for his morning draught, an eminent-looking group came filing out of the cathedral and paused near the stall in brisk discussion, pointing up at decrepit features of the fabric. There had been scaffolding standing for months, indecisive, while the authorities bickered about what needed to be done.

She recognized the Dean, Dr Sancroft, a commanding figure, always greeted with immense respect when he sailed across the churchyard. "That's the Bishop with him," Grandfather whispered, "and Mr Slingsby behind them – *he's*

9

Master of the Mint." He named others, Mr Chichele, a Member of Parliament, and Mr May, the famous architect.

"And your own Mr Evelyn," she said.

John Evelyn was a very pleasant gentleman from Deptford and an occasional customer. He did not ignore her as some did, but treated her as a lady. He was some sort of government commissioner, with a passion for collecting books and prints. Even today he managed to throw them a friendly smile. He was talking earnestly to a younger man.

"I entirely agree with you, Dr Wren—"

"It would be penny wise and pound foolish to repair the steeple on the old foundation. It needs a new one. Some people think of nothing but saving money, patching things up. If we could have a clean sweep, produce new plans, build something worthy—"

"Could we not submit a new plan, with an estimate?"

"The King would back us. But I know what the committee would say." Dr Wren laughed bitterly. "That I'm only a professor of astronomy – with my head among the stars!"

Dr Sancroft was beckoning. The whole party obediently trooped after him towards the Deanery.

"The church is certainly in a sad state," said Grandfather. "We can look forward to dust and noise for months, I suppose – perhaps years."

"I think Mr Evelyn's friend would like to pull the whole place down—"

"Dr Wren? Oh, these young men have the wildest notions."

A few weeks later she was to remember that conversation. But now, as Grandfather went off to the tavern, her mind turned to other things.

Rather reluctantly the old man always displayed a little pile of cheap pamphlets and broadsides dealing with recent events – some particularly gory murder, the scaffold speech of a criminal, or rather improper but very amusing verses

10

about some courtier's scandalous love-affairs. Sarah was shy of being caught reading them but made no great effort to resist the temptation.

This morning she became so immersed in the horrific details of *The Tyburn Ghost* that she did not notice the boy's arrival until his shadow fell across the page.

She looked up guiltily, then felt a spasm of pleasure when she saw who it was. Instantly she became the attentive bookseller at the customer's service. But this customer seemed in no need of attention. He was already happily absorbed. He had a cloak over his arm, a fine one, velvet-lined, new and spotless. He laid it carelessly across the other books. She felt piqued that, after yesterday, he had not spoken to her. She said, ironically:

"And a very good morning to *you*, sir! You find it cold?"

He looked up, thoughts obviously far away. "Cold?"

"Your cloak! When everyone is sweltering."

"Oh, *that*? It isn't mine." He need not have told her. No boy would own a splendid garment like that.

"No?" She mocked him, acting surprise.

"My fool of a master left it in a tavern last night. We went to the Devil—"

She burst out laughing. "You went to the devil?"

"The tavern," he explained patiently. "Along Fleet Street. By Temple Bar. I have to attend him – with a torch to guide his faltering footsteps! And I can tell you, he needs me, coming back. He forgot his cloak, so of course I'm blamed. And this morning I'm sent back—"

"All that way! In this heat!" She was sympathetic.

"The distance is nothing. Back home—" To her disappointment he broke off without saying where 'home' was. She could tell that he was country-born. His speech was pleasant but a shade outlandish. Not from any of the counties near London.

"But a long way to go for a drink," she said.

"One meets useful people at the Devil." His lip curled. "It's kept by *Alderman* Barford, no less. My master fancies wearing a scarlet gown like his. So – we must go to the Devil though there are scores of taverns nearer. And he must show off his new cloak, though the night air was like an oven. And I must attend him as link-boy, in livery, with a little sword, no more use than a child's toy." He stopped. "I mustn't gossip about my employer. I should be thankful, in these days, that I've got a place."

He turned to his book again with an air of finality. She busied herself dusting and straightening the stock, humming a tune under her breath. She sold a volume of sermons to a parson and answered an enquiry for a playbook. After these few months she had built up a good working knowledge of authors and titles and editions.

Another youth paused at the stall and leafed through some old chronicles. His face was familiar and she knew he was most unlikely to buy. The churchyard was a happy hunting-ground for pickpockets, confidence tricksters and thieves of every kind. He was one of them.

Grandfather had warned her to be on her guard but not worry unduly. "Such people don't steal books," he said, "because they can't easily sell them again. It's mostly *good* men who steal books – books they long to possess but haven't the money to buy." They stole to keep, not to sell on, as professional thieves did. There was no quick market for stolen books. "And," said Mr Calamy realistically, "those who keep get caught."

A costly cloak was more marketable. Sarah felt uneasy when another familiar local character appeared on the footboy's other side. This was Becky, who sold oranges – formerly in the playhouses but, until they reopened, wherever else she could find customers. A cheerful, cheeky wench, no better than she should be (Grandfather hinted) and certainly no book-lover. Sarah doubted if she could even read. This interest in the stall was improbable. When she exchanged a meaning glance with the thief, Sarah's uneasiness hardened into suspicion.

It constantly happened in the churchyard. A decoy would distract the intended victim. A smart pickpocket could carry out his work in seconds and vanish in the crowd before the victim discovered his loss. And against the decoy there would be no evidence whatever.

Normally a mere apprentice or footboy was not worth robbing. But the cloak, the handsome velvet-lined cloak, was a different matter. Sarah became increasingly anxious as she watched the two accomplices edge into position on either side of her new acquaintance.

How could she warn the footboy without the thieves realizing she had done so? The problem – and the thought of the possible results to herself – chilled her blood. These folks always got their own back in the end. Stallholders found it safest to turn a blind eye, for anyone working here regularly was virtually defenceless. She knew what could be done to her and her grandfather. Even if they escaped violence their stock might well be set fire to during the night. The fellowship of thieves would close ranks to teach them a lesson.

Any stallholder was vulnerable. None more so than a girl – or that girl's old grandfather. She shuddered as she measured the possible consequences.

Yet, if she did nothing, there would be repercussions for the boy. What had he said, with such feeling, only a few minutes ago? "I should be thankful, in these days, that I've got a place." How long would he keep that place if he let his master's cloak be stolen? How could he explain and justify the circumstances in which he had lost it?

No, she thought desperately, somehow she must think of

a way to put him on his guard without giving the thieves a hint that she had warned him.

She went on humming, straightening the layout of the books, covertly watching the trio on the other side of the stall. If only the country boy would look up and meet her eye! But he was obstinately absorbed in his reading. She must on no account meet the eyes of the other two, who were edging their way closer to converge upon him. She saw them exchange a second significant glance behind his back. The thief's hand crept stealthily towards the hem of the outspread cloak. Any moment now the orange-girl would create some distraction, the boy would turn to her, and in a flash both thief and cloak would be gone.

The whole situation could have taken only a minute or two to develop. The solution came in a matter of seconds.

Yesterday she had envied the boy his knowledge of Latin. If only she could have murmured a warning in that language! She searched her memory for the few words her grandfather had taught her. The dog's name in Latin would have been *puer*. She herself would have been a *puella*, a girl. And in Rome, Grandfather joked, they would have had the words cut in the doorstep, *cave canem*, "beware of the dog".

It was enough. To speak the words would have made her warning obvious. She changed her humming to a casual song, carefully articulating those precious few words that would mean nothing to the two accomplices but must surely impinge on the boy's consciousness and awaken him to the realization of what was happening.

Beware of the girl, beware of the boy . . .

It worked. His mind reacted as quickly as her own. The orange-girl was a fraction too late in her intervention. The footboy had already swung round the other way, seen the thief's hand fasten on the edge of the cloak and start to draw it away.

"Hi! You let go of that!"

Sarah heard the crack of the clenched fist on the thief's jaw. He howled, staggered back, releasing the cloak, and was off like a startled alley-cat.

"What a thing!" cried the orange-girl, all innocence. She strolled away, beginning to cry her wares.

The footboy gathered up the cloak and hung it over his arm. He smiled gratefully – almost incredulously – across at Sarah. "You know Latin!"

"Hardly."

"Actually you'd got the grammar wrong – that was what really startled me out of my reading. But it was clever of you. I understood what you were trying to tell me."

He does not mean to be patronizing, she thought, he just can't believe that a girl could know any Latin.

"So long as we understand each other," she said coolly. And went on with her dusting, vigorously.

# 3

After that their friendship ripened.

In different ways they both needed it. It was not hard to see each other most days. She was often alone at the stall and his errands gave him frequent excuses to pass by. He seemed a serious youth. Was he, she wondered, rather *solemn*, too ready always to bury his nose in a book? But one day he suddenly exploded into laughter.

"May I see?" she said.

He held out the open book, *The Anatomie of Abuses*, by Philip Stubbes, a Puritan in Elizabeth's reign. "*For as concerning football playing,*" she read, "*I protest unto you it may rather be called a friendly kind of fight, than a play or recreation; a bloody and murdering practice, than a fellowly sport or pastime. For doth not everyone lie in wait for his adversary, so that by this means sometimes their necks are broken, sometimes their backs, sometimes one part thrust out of joint, sometime another, sometime their noses gush out with blood, sometime their eyes start out . . .*"

She smiled. "I thought there was a ball."

He wiped his eyes. "Sometime – as Mr Stubbes would say – one forgets the ball."

"And did *you* behave like this?"

"Sometime! We were not so rough."

"I'm glad you survived." She meant it. Though she privately thought this sport incomprehensible she was relieved to know he was much like other boys.

Hugh always made himself scarce when her grandfather

returned. For all his poor eyesight Mr Calamy was well aware of the youth's existence. Neighbouring stallholders had dropped hints. Grandfather was not best pleased. One evening, over supper, he tackled Sarah.

"This lad, who haunts our stall – who is he?"

"His name is Hugh Falconer. He loves books—"

"It's the books, is it? What do you know of him?"

"Not much. He's footboy to a Mr Biddulph."

"I don't know any Mr Biddulph."

"Very likely not, Grandad. He doesn't sound as if he'd buy books. He's a fishmonger. Big house above Billingsgate. Fish Street Hill."

"He may be respectable enough," Grandfather conceded reluctantly, though clearly an indifference to books was a black mark against him. "Boys are another matter. Boys who hang about in the churchyard. You're over young for boys."

That stung her. "I must have *some* friends."

"Well, I suppose . . . but don't neglect your work."

She certainly did not do that. She always broke off any talk with Hugh if a customer appeared.

The youth was impressed by her knowledge of the stock, but clearly puzzled that a girl should possess so much. "I expect Mr Calamy has taught you?"

"Yes, but not everything. I learned about books when I was little. Long before I came to help him here."

She described how her mother used to take her to visit Great-uncle William at his elegant house in Covent Garden. Memories flooded back. The grand rooms with their gleaming chandeliers and lofty plaster ceilings. The delicious cakes from the pastrycook's. Her great-uncle was unmarried, there seemed to be no maids or serving-women, only his two menservants. It was odd, though – once she had picked up a lady's slipper from under a cabinet. Great-uncle William

17

had whisked it away in a flash, laughing so much that he went quite red in the face.

Most of all she remembered the books, rows and rows of them. She had been allowed to look at some of them, and turn the great globe on its pedestal, tracing with her finger the voyages her father had made.

It had all ended abruptly, she told Hugh, just when she was becoming a fluent reader. Grandfather disapproved of his younger brother. One day he told her mother that these visits must cease.

"At first I could not understand." Sarah could laugh now at her own ignorance. "I thought he meant that poor Uncle Will *had* a loose liver. I imagined it somehow bobbing about inside him! Till Mother explained that he *was* a loose liver. 'Your wicked Uncle Will,' she called him. But to me," she ended sadly, "he was very good."

Had she talked too much about herself? She wished that this boy would be more forthcoming in return. On later occasions she managed, by degrees, to loosen his tongue. There were emotions, she sensed, that had been bottled up too long.

His voice was unsteady when he spoke of home, the apple orchards, the river where he swam with his friends, the long wall of the distant Welsh hills, black against the orange sunset.

Why had he left all that and come to London? "You say your father has a farm?"

"Ay. But too few acres – and too many sons."

"So, you had to . . ." She paused, afraid to make him touchy.

He reassured her. "I left willingly enough. The schoolmaster summed me up. He told Dad, 'Your Hugh's the sort who'll always want to see what's over the next hill.' "

"And what did your dad say?"

Hugh chuckled. "He said, 'That's fine – if you don't mind a stiff climb to start with.' "

He owed a lot to that schoolmaster. The man had seen that, though he played and fought like the other lads, he had more curiosity and a taste for books that marked him out. The schoolmaster had written to a printer friend in London. This friend had offered a seven-year apprenticeship. Hugh's father had reckoned that he could manage the money and the indentures had been signed according to the law.

"And you came up here alone? All this way? By coach?"

"We'd no money for that. I walked."

He had worked his way with the drovers. They were the men, he explained, who brought the cattle and sheep across country to the butchers' market at Smithfield. Many came from the heart of Wales, following the broad grass tracks that had been trodden for centuries.

"It took time. Twelve miles a day was the limit. We couldn't drive the beasts too hard – no good getting them to London with no meat on their bones."

"And at night?"

"There were regular stopping places, with grazing for the stock and good inns that welcomed drovers." His eyes shone as he remembered the Feathers at Ledbury, where they had rested the stock before they faced the steep climb over the Malvern Hills. It had been good at Broadway, too, before they crossed the Cotswolds. There was a wide grassy street through the village with space for hundreds of animals. The drovers took turns to watch at night and he'd done his shift with the rest.

"Most of the men were armed," he said.

"Against cattle-thieves?"

"Not so much that. Some of them were carrying money for their masters, to pay over to people in London.

19

Thousands of pounds, could be. They were grand, those drovers! Scholars, some of them – you'd have been surprised. And the tales they could tell—"

"I've never been ten miles from London," she said wistfully. "All my life."

"You will," he promised her. She could not imagine how.

It had taken almost two weeks to reach the Chilterns, the last range of hills. Far off he had seen the pearly haze of London's smoke stretched like a hem to the eastern sky.

The story took almost as long to tell. It came out in disconnected fragments on different days, frequently interrupted. She pieced it together as best she could. Long afterwards he was surprised at her vivid memory. "I can remember what interests me," she said.

London had been no disappointment. Mr Jackson's printshop, in a poky court off Fleet Street, was a cheerful, noisy place. Mrs Jackson was motherly. The apprentices were fed well and treated as family. The work was hard. Mr Jackson was conscientious in his training.

Sarah knew plenty about books but not the methods that produced them. She understood words like quarto and octavo, but Hugh had to explain how they derived from the way big sheets of paper were folded and cut into pages of varying sizes. The typefaces were often named after the printer who had first designed them, like the Frenchman, Christopher Plantin. Mr Jackson even had founts of Greek and Hebrew type. Then there were the illustrations, woodcuts and engravings and—"What a lot to master!" she said, and felt him warm to her admiration.

"Mr Jackson said I was quick. But I know I'd have needed those other six years—" He broke off, his face clouding as he remembered.

Early last summer the plague struck. Trade fell off. King

and court fled from the city. So did most people of quality. The theatres closed. Shutters went up everywhere. Mr Jackson had a major work in hand, a three-volume history, to keep his press busy. They worked on until, within a month, the sickness claimed him.

The quarantine rules kept them all prisoners in the house for weeks. Mercifully no one else was infected. But when the period was up Hugh found himself homeless and masterless. "Wouldn't some other printer take over your apprenticeship?" Sarah asked.

He shook his head. "In ordinary times maybe the Stationers Company would have arranged something. But everything was in chaos. Other printers were dying, or they'd quit London. It was like the end of the world."

She had lived through it herself. "But," she said with a spasm of envy, "*you* still had your parents. You could go home."

"And maybe carry the infection with me? Or have everybody afraid I should? They stoned people who'd come out of London. They had pickets outside towns like Oxford, turning them back. I'd never have got halfway to Herefordshire. And I didn't want to give up that easy. I vowed I'd stick it out somehow."

Somehow he had. Sleeping rough in the half-deserted city. Doing any odd job to put food in his belly.

"My best time was milking a cow when the usual girl took sick. The cow was kept in a shed off Cheapside, but I used to shut my eyes and picture the Black Mountains stretched along the horizon." He laughed. "Then I had to open them and hawk my pail of milk around the streets."

With winter the plague began to slacken off. He had looked for more settled employment.

"Maybe I was stupid, but I'd nobody to advise me. I thought that any skilled trade would mean another apprenticeship, starting all over again. I couldn't ask my dad to stump up for a second premium."

"So that's why—"

"Why I'm footboy to Would-be Alderman Ezra Biddulph."

He would not say much about life on Fish Street Hill. He was no whiner, but his occasional indignation would flash out like lightning. She read between the lines. Mr Biddulph was clearly a pompous fool, his wife a strait-laced scold. The footman was a brute, the cook had a rough tongue but a kind enough heart. Of the three maids, Ellen was the prettiest but empty-headed. Hugh was the lowest of the low, and made to feel it. He did not mind so much the menial tasks – "A farmer's son is used to muck!" he said tersely – but he did not like the humiliations Biddulph laid upon him.

"Such as?"

He hesitated. "It's Saturday. So tonight I must kneel down with a basin of water and wash his feet. Then I must cut his toenails. If he ate less he could bend down and do that for himself." She murmured sympathy, struggling a little to keep a straight face. "Then," he went on, "I must stand behind his chair with lighted candles and search his head for nits!"

"Ugh! How hateful for you! After the printshop—"

"I shall survive. It's a relief talking to you. But here comes your grandfather. I'd best be on my way."

She watched till she saw him vanish in the crowd. She did not know that they would never stand chatting there again.

# 4

"You'd best look out," Ellen warned Hugh as he entered the kitchen. "The master's been asking for you."

"He's in a foul temper," said the cook.

That was not unusual. He felt no special alarm. The fishmonger never timed him on his errands. "I'd best go up then. I've brought the letter he wanted." He hurried up the stairs but paused outside the parlour. The voices within were strident.

"I always meet my friends on a Saturday! Why—"

Mrs Biddulph cut in, her voice thin as vinegar. "After Saturday night comes Sunday morning. I will not have my husband stumbling as we go up the aisle. Or snoring in the pew when the preacher is not ten minutes into his sermon."

"It is important to meet my friends. My standing in the City depends on it!"

"Then meet them at other times. Monday to Friday should be enough. It will do more for your standing in the City if you can appear decent and sober on the Sabbath."

Hugh listened with glee. There was something to be said for the acid-tongued Mrs Biddulph. He could scarcely intrude upon them.

"I'll not be dictated to by my own wife!" declared Mr Biddulph.

"Then you will walk up the aisle without a wife at your side. And that will do no good to your 'standing in the City'."

"You'll have to attend service yourself—"

"I can go to another church. There are one or two notable new preachers I would like to hear. It does not matter where one attends service – except that a man like you, who wishes to rise in the world, is wiser to be regular in his own parish."

Her husband could answer only with a kind of wordless explosion. He flung open the door so abruptly that Hugh had barely time to wipe the grin off his face.

"*You!* And about time!" It was clearly a relief to turn on someone who dared not answer back.

"I had to wait, sir, until Mr Shelton wrote the letter." He held it out, folded and sealed.

Mr Biddulph snatched it. "I have told you before – you should bring my letters on a tray." He ran his eye over the message, snorted, and thrust it into his pocket. "And what were you doing in Paul's Churchyard? It wasn't on your way."

That was unanswerable. In his early days with the fishmonger he had always prepared himself for such a question. Lately, being unchallenged, he had grown careless.

Mr Biddulph did not wait for an answer. "I'm going to get to the bottom of this." He marched down the passage to the small back room where Hugh normally waited upon him with hot water, clean linen and highly polished shoes. There was a bed there into which he sometimes had to help his employer when Mrs Biddulph had bolted her door against him.

"Now—" Mr Biddulph turned. Though he had not recovered his good humour he was happier in this new situation which he could dominate. "You go to the churchyard to meet a wench. Don't deny it. Pearse saw you. He tells me it is not the first time." So, thought Hugh, the footman had been telling tales. "I will not have it," Mr Biddulph continued. "You are too young for wenching. You are a member of my household." He puffed out his cheeks importantly. "I am responsible for your moral welfare. I am – dammit, what's the word?"

"*In loco parentis?*" Hugh exclaimed with instinctive helpfulness. "Latin for 'in the place of a parent'."

Mr Biddulph did not appear grateful for his assistance. "Conceited young monkey! I won't have you getting mixed up with some slut."

That was more than Hugh could stand. "She's not a slut! She helps her grandfather at his stall – and *he's* a member of the Stationers Company. I sometimes speak to her – about books – as I pass by—"

"When you should be about *my* business. I don't pay your wages to waste *my* time in Paul's Churchyard chasing wenches. Talking about books indeed! Why should you want to talk about *books*?"

Thus challenged Hugh could not resist the temptation to tell him. "Because I miss them! If things had gone differently I shouldn't be here, in a house where nobody ever opens a book—"

"You're insolent. You neglect your duties. You lie to me—"

"I don't!"

"You contradict me!" That statement at least could hardly be contradicted. "You're on a fair way to damnation. A wench! I know you boys!" He seized a stick. "I'm going to beat the devil out of you."

"I'll not be beaten, sir."

Hugh stood there, flushed and defiant, hands clenched with determination.

"You defy me?"

"I'll not be beaten."

Purple face twitching, Mr Biddulph raised his stick.

Hugh grabbed it and twisted. There was a struggle. The

stick leapt from his master's grip and went spinning on to the bed.

Mr Biddulph strode to the door, opened it, and bellowed: "Pearse!" He wheeled round on Hugh. "You are dismissed. Don't ask for a reference, you'll get none. Or only one that'll make certain you never find a post in the City again."

The footman appeared, leering as he took in the situation. "You called, sir?"

"I've dismissed Falconer. Idleness, lying, insolence – and now violence! He'll leave at once and never set foot in this house again."

"I'll see he don't, sir!" Pearse sounded confident. He had gained his position for his formidable size.

"One moment, though. I'd promised him a good hiding. No one can say I'm not a man of my word. Shut the door, Pearse. Now, Falconer. Drop your breeches."

If Hugh had needed anything to strengthen his resolve that order would have been enough. "I'll not be beaten. I'm not a child!"

Mr Biddulph picked up his stick. He nodded to the footman. Pearse sprang forward, clutched at Hugh's waistline and tugged violently. There was a tearing sound as the hooks burst away which secured breeches to doublet. Hugh twisted free, jabbing his fist into the man's stomach. With his other hand he grabbed desperately at his breeches. They were sagging, but they kept up.

Pearse barred his escape, hungry for revenge, panting suggestions. "If we tied his wrists to the bedposts, sir, and his ankles too – spreadeagled as they do in the Navy, sir—"

"Excellent! I'm not going to beat him in his livery. That material cost me a pretty penny."

Later, telling the story, Hugh could share in the laughter.

"He was quite prepared to beat my backside like a raw steak – but he wasn't going to spoil his precious livery!" At the time, though, the situation looked grim. He read the ferocity in both their faces.

"If I'm already dismissed," he protested, "you've no right—"

"He talks like a lawyer," said Mr Biddulph. "Watch him. I'll call down for some cord." He opened the door.

Mrs Biddulph stood framed there, majestic. "What on earth is happening?" Her husband stepped back as she swept in. "I'm going to teach this young scoundrel—" he began.

Hugh saw his chance.

"Stop!" thundered Mr Biddulph.

But Hugh was through the doorway, with Pearse after him, clattering down the stairs. Hugh fumbled as he opened the street-door and with a cry of triumph the footman overtook him. Hugh kicked his shins. A moment later he was in the street, gasping as he raced clumsily up the cobbled hill, frantically clutching at his loose breeches. Behind him the heavy door banged. Risking a glance back he saw that Pearse was no longer in pursuit. No doubt he would smugly assure the Biddulphs that their footboy had been duly ejected.

What now, Hugh wondered? He could not go back. Where *could* he go? As he stood there, regaining his breath and trying to gather his wits, he saw Ellen come out of the alley that led to the kitchen-door. She saw him, signalled, and hurried up the hill.

"Oh, *Hugh*! What a thing!" Her voice and face registered shock, sympathy and pleasurable excitement.

"I'm not going back!"

"Don't blame you! But you can't go like this—"

"Like what?"

"In your livery, silly! It's Mr Biddulph's property. He

could have you for theft. He'd have you just where he wants you."

He saw that. "How else can I go? In my shirt? If I step inside that house again—"

"Oh, you mustn't! I've a better idea. Wait for me in the yard of the Star. I'll bundle up your own things and bring them up to you. You can change in the stables. I'll be back in no time."

She went. He had thought her pretty but empty-headed. He had done her an injustice. Soft-hearted she certainly was.

He waited in the inn yard. Ostlers and stable-lads were bustling about. On Saturday evenings the place was full of life and he got many a friendly nod, for he was often sent here to fetch ale for the servants' table. Within a few minutes Ellen was back. The house was still in an uproar, she reported gleefully, with master and mistress engaged in a mighty row upstairs, while the maids delighted in the drama and giggled at the footman's discomfiture.

Only the cook knew what Ellen was up to. "She sent you this slice of pasty – you'll miss your supper." There was no time to discuss his future. He disappeared into an empty stable, changed swiftly, and emerged with the black and gold-laced garments neatly folded.

"I can say I found them on the doorstep," she said.

"And thank Cook." He smiled at her. "And you – you've been very kind."

"I'll miss you, Hugh." Impulsively she dropped the livery on a convenient mounting-block and flung her arms round him. Luckily he no longer had to worry about the insecurity of his breeches and his hands were free to return her hug as warmly as it deserved. Yes, she *was* soft-hearted, Ellen was. Her lips too, as she clamped them enthusiastically over his startled mouth.

"We should ha' done that before," she said regretfully as she let him go.

An old ostler smiled benevolently at their parting. "Ah, well," he told them, "ye're only young once."

# 5

It would soon be dark. It was time to take stock. He counted his money. A shilling and twopence, all he possessed in the world. He had not a friend in London on whose door he could knock for shelter. After Mr Jackson's death his family had left Fleet Street.

He glanced round the inn yard. There was stabling for dozens of horses. Who would notice if he bedded down in one of the haylofts for tonight?

Choosing his moment he climbed a ladder and crept into the sweet-smelling new-mown hay. It took him back to those golden days and nights on the drove-roads. He could fancy himself at some Cotswold or Chiltern halting-place. The distant voices singing in the taproom helped the illusion. "Happy days," he murmured to himself, and, being drained of emotion by the events of the past few hours, he slipped into unconsciousness.

He dreamed – a ravel of confused dreams, without ends or beginnings. His old drover friends came into them, their unshaven faces and their nicknames, Bucket-belly, who gulped down ale as a horse drank water, and the Bonfire Man, whose prodigious pipe filled a room with tobacco fumes and emptied it of people. In Hugh's dream the smoke was thicker than ever. He woke, coughing and choking. The smoke was real. There was urgent shouting in the yard below. One voice rang clear above the tumult.

"Never mind Pudding Lane! We've enough to do here."

Horses were whinnying, iron-shod hoofs stamping on the

cobbles, men yelling and swearing as they tried to master the panic-stricken beasts.

Hugh was up in an instant, groping for the bundle that had been his pillow, thrusting his arms through the straps. Then it was down the ladder and out into the yard. In the dense smoke men showed as grotesque shadows. There was a roar and a mighty *whoosh!* as the thatched roof of an outhouse flared up like a gigantic torch.

He had seen farm fires and at first this seemed no different. Everyone helped as best he could. A voice of authority was calling: "Get the beasts out, or we can't do anything! Can someone hold this brute for me—"

Hugh was handy. The horse was dancing in its terror. "Can I, sir?"

"Can you handle him? He's big—"

"I'm used to horses—"

"Good. Take him up the street after the others."

Hugh seized the halter. It was almost jerked out of his hand as the great head tossed skywards. Somehow he hung on, somehow dodged those perilous hoofs. Then the old knack reasserted itself. The quivering mountain of horse-flesh seemed to draw comfort from the insignificant manikin stroking and murmuring at its side. Out in the street the air was clearer. The darkness flooded back. Only the sky above the rooftops was flushed an angry red.

The file of horses calmed as they were led up the street. One of the stable-men took charge at the top and got them tethered in a disused yard. Windows were opening everywhere, candles gleaming, voices calling down.

"Where's the fire?"

"Pudding Lane – Farriner's bakehouse—"

"Then the King's bread will be burnt this morning!" There was a burst of laughter. Thomas Farriner supplied bread to the Palace.

31

A woman's voice, more sympathetic, shouted from a bedroom: "Are they all safe?"

Someone answered: "The Farriners got out across the roof. Their maid was trapped, poor lass."

Someone was explaining that the east wind must have blown sparks across the intervening buildings. The straw in the inn yard had caught fire. It had been vital to get the horses out.

No cause for alarm. The leather buckets that always hung in the porch at St Magnus were being fetched. With fire-hooks and ladders, and plenty of willing hands to use them, the blaze would soon be under control. "You can all go back to bed," a man called reassuringly to the nightcapped faces above.

Hugh had no bed to go back to and excitement had banished all thought of further sleep. A clock struck three. It would be daylight in another hour or two. He was uncomfortably close to Mr Biddulph's house and at any moment he might encounter Pearse among this crowd of sightseers. It seemed wise to slip round the corner into Pudding Lane.

There was an even denser throng outside the Farriners' bakehouse. There was no saving the old building, which was mainly wood except for the stonework of the chimney and the ovens. Once the beams forming its framework burnt through it would collapse upon itself.

There was keen argument among the neighbours lest the flames should spread to their own properties. Some wanted to demolish a thatched roof which was an obvious risk. The owner objected vehemently. "There are buckets, aren't there?"

Plenty, someone agreed, but where was the water to fill them? So many wells were dry. The public conduits in the surrounding streets were no better. There was the river, true, but at this stage of the tide it would take scores of men to make a long enough chain to reach the foreshore.

A fire-break would be better. "You want a clear gap between the buildings," was one suggestion.

"*I* don't. It's *my* house!" The owner swore ferociously.

There was a clatter of hoofs from the top end of the lane. The crowd parted as pikemen shoved them back. The Lord Mayor had arrived. Sir Thomas Bludworth did not look best pleased to be roused from his bed at this hour. He surveyed the scene with some impatience.

The bakehouse chose that moment to collapse, transforming itself into a gigantic bonfire from which the chimney pointed heavenwards like a finger of doom. For some minutes there was hope that the worst was over. But, as the breeze fanned the ashes, they would suddenly glow ruby with new life. A charred beam would dart out a tongue of fresh flame. The Lord Mayor's horse danced with terror. The bystanders backed away hurriedly. There were more demands for a fire-break.

Sir Thomas made light of the danger. "To call me out for this! There are always fires. Any old woman could put this out by herself!" He won some laughter, but there were cries of resentment as he wheeled his horse and rode away. To those who lived in the neighbourhood it was no joking matter.

Before the discussion of a fire-break could be resumed there was a fresh diversion. A heavy cask, mounted on wheels, was being trundled noisily down the hill. Two men cleared its path importantly, the parish fire-squirts gleaming in their hands. Hugh stared at this equipment, for a moment with hope and then with less confidence. The squirts were hollow brass cylinders, no more than two feet long with a half-inch aperture. The water had to be pumped from the cask – which took three men – and though for a few moments a thin jet shot hissing into the flames it quickly died back to a dribble and ceased. After all this effort the device delivered barely a gallon at a time.

The fire-hooks looked more promising. They were fitted to stout poles, twenty or thirty feet long, with ropes running through iron rings. Once the hook was firmly fixed over the roofbeam of a building, and the ropes pulled by a gang of strong men – or horses, better still – a brief struggle would bring the beam tumbling down, the tiles or thatch disintegrating as it came.

Hugh had not the weight to compete with the full-grown men hauling on the ropes but his help was welcomed when some draught-horses arrived. He was quickly sized up as a handy lad who could control these stumbling, snorting beasts. He worked tirelessly until, their task accomplished, they became an obstacle to the householders trying to carry their goods to safety. Heavy pieces of furniture were getting jammed in doorways or on stairs. Heaps of bedding were flopping from upper windows. Old folks and invalids were being carried bodily.

Hugh, looking round for some further chance to be useful, saw a young woman clutching her tearful child on one hip and striving with her free hand to carry a clock. "Can I take that for you?" he said.

"Oh, if you *would*—"

Before he had gone ten paces a hand was clapped on his shoulder and a furious face thrust into his own. "*I'll* take that, young man!"

"He's helping me, Mother," the younger woman protested.

"Himself, more like! You got to watch out, my girl. There's all sorts about at a time like this. Handing that clock to a perfect stranger!"

Hugh kept his temper and, for the moment, the clock. "If you'll tell me where you want it taken—"

"Very well – but don't expect—"

He had expected nothing. Under her suspicious eye he carried the clock up the lane and set it down on the doorstep she indicated. Behind them the young mother shouted her thanks. But before he was out of earshot the older woman was rebuking her for her innocence in trusting a youth she did not know from Adam.

Mr Biddulph had already called him a liar. Now he was suspected of being a thief. He was furious, but fair-minded enough to remember his own experience in the churchyard. There were plenty of rogues about, especially at a scene of disaster like this one.

He felt a sudden anxiety for the safety of his own bundle. He had slipped it off his shoulders to leave himself freer. He thrust his way through the crowd and, to his relief, found it just where he had put it down. As he stooped over it he heard the voice of the woman who had previously challenged him.

"Is that yours?" she demanded suspiciously.

"Yes," he said between his teeth. "It's about the only thing that is."

Suddenly he realized how exhausted he was. He was no longer needed here. Others, luckier people who still had homes of their own, were beginning to drift away. He would walk just far enough to get out of the noise and smoke, then crawl into some corner and try to snatch another hour of sleep.

He turned west along Thames Street. It ran parallel with the river, separated by a strip of low-lying ground built over with decrepit warehouses and dwellings. Dark alleys led to the wharves and the landing stairs where watermen picked up their passengers. It was lucky that the fire had not broken

35

out in this quarter, with its serried rows of tar-barrels and stacks of Scandinavian timber.

Day was breaking. He looked back. The dawn was masked by the smoke-cloud over the rooftops. Only London Bridge stood clear, marching across the water on its nineteen narrow arches. He could see the rotting heads of the traitors impaled on their high tower at the Southwark end. Looking, at this distance, like ghastly pins. Turning hastily, he faced the westward skyline, pricked with other towers and church spires, catching the first gleams of morning.

In a few hours all the bells would be ringing, calling the godly – and the not so godly – to worship. Well, he thought with some satisfaction, if Mr Biddulph paraded to St Margaret's this morning he might or might not have Mrs Biddulph at his side, but he would certainly have no liveried footboy walking behind with his prayer-book on a cushion.

Church! That prompted a thought. There would be shelter in a church, in its porch at least if its door was still locked. He could rest undisturbed until service time. He walked on, the tang of burnt wood on the air gradually fading. The looming bulk of Baynards Castle showed that he was nearing Puddle Dock where the River Fleet would bar his way. He would try the next church he saw.

He was in luck. Its door was not locked. He tiptoed in, feet leaden with weariness, and slipped into a pew at one side. It was not so soft as the hay, but he had reached the stage when that did not matter.

# 6

Waking that morning, Sarah found the sky muffled in a dirty blanket of cloud. It was disappointing. At supper her grandfather had talked of taking her upriver to Westminster. It would be cooler on the water, out of the stifling streets. Now the long-needed rain must be coming at just the wrong moment.

It was not, however, a rain-cloud. "It's smoke," said Fanny, poking her head round the door. "A fire. Down Billingsgate way."

"It must be a big one."

"It is. Mary woke up at two o'clock. She saw the flames and got me out of bed to see. All red the sky was. Terrible."

"It's burning still."

"The ashes often smoulder for days. Thank the Lord it wasn't us."

There were always fires in some part of the city, and would be till folk took more heed of the building regulations. Mr Evelyn said that the King himself had warned the authorities, but even he had not been able to budge them. Mr Evelyn had told Grandfather that there would be a disaster one day. He was a great one for worrying about problems.

Meanwhile, as Fanny said, this fire was a long way off and they all had their own work to do. And church to attend, thought Sarah. She opened the press and took out her best clothes for the occasion. Outside, it was fine and sunny, the

37

sky blue except for that sullen grey smoke in the east.

On the way to church all the neighbours were exchanging rumours. Gossip was usually kept till after the service, a permissible relaxation after the long sermon. Until then you were supposed to fix your thoughts on higher things and you exchanged only conventional bows and greetings. Today it was impossible to pretend that you were not thinking of the fire. Presumably it had been put out by now.

We shall simply recite the General Confession more guiltily than usual, Sarah reflected, and the Thanksgiving with extra fervour. She used to think a lot, sitting demurely beside Grandfather – and at many other times too. He urged her always to read books with a critical mind and she was apt to apply his advice to life in general. She often wondered how she could have sinned so badly in the past week as to make her a "miserable offender" with "no health" in her. She was seldom miserable and her health was excellent. Where was she going wrong?

Today she followed Grandfather decorously up the aisle, head meekly bowed, glancing neither to right nor to left. So it was not until a full hour later that, with a start of incredulity, she caught sight of Hugh Falconer.

He sat alone in one of the side pews, shadowed by a stone pillar. Those pews were seldom occupied now. Since the pestilence the congregation was much reduced.

He was making himself as unobtrusive as possible, sitting very low in his seat. Indeed, strictly speaking, he was not sitting at all. He was tilted over against the pillar. Gracious! He was *asleep*. Hugh! How could he? But that dark head was unmistakable.

What on earth was he doing here anyhow? In *her* church? With a brief spasm of delicious vanity – now there was sin for you! – she toyed with the attractive notion that it was because of her own charms. Boys were known to do such

38

things. But no one had ever done so for her. On further reflection it was not very flattering if this one had fallen asleep. Calm reason came to her aid. Hugh would not have known which church she attended. For the remaining half-hour of the sermon it was difficult to concentrate on the preacher.

When he concluded, and she glanced across at Hugh, she was relieved to see that he had been roused by the general stirring of the congregation and was on his feet like the rest.

Somehow she must snatch a word with him outside. No doubt a well-bred girl would have let him make the first move, but she was eaten up with curiosity and could not let him sneak away without a word. Grandfather always paused outside to greet friends and compare notes on the sermon.

She looked across again as they filed out after the blessing, hoping to catch his eye. He had vanished. Surely he could not have pushed his way out in front of all these important people? No, he had merely shrunk back into the shadow of the pillar.

She followed her grandfather out into the sunshine. Then, once he was safely caught up in sociability, she slipped back into the church. The old beadle was thundering angrily: "Up to no good, I'll be bound! Come out of it, you!" Hugh emerged sheepishly.

She caught her breath as she saw what had not been visible before. Red-rimmed eyes stared from a black-grimed face. His shirt was scorched and filthy. She told him afterwards, "You looked like a fiend from Hell."

Now, though, she sailed in to the rescue. "*Hugh!*"

The beadle swung round. "You know this young ruffian, miss?"

"He's not a ruffian. He's . . . most respectable. But, Hugh, how did you get like this? What are you doing here?"

"Just what I was asking, miss!"

"I—" Hugh began, then stopped with a gasp as he looked down at his soot-streaked hands and dishevelled clothing. "I was helping at the fire. Then I came in here – I must have fallen asleep—"

"You must!" She turned to the beadle. "I know him, Mr Lewis. I'll look after him. It will be all right."

"If you say so, miss." The old man sounded doubtful.

"We must get you cleaned up, Hugh. You can't go back to Fish Street Hill like this."

He gulped. "I can't go back at all. Ever."

She gave him a keen look. There was a story here, but this was not the time or place for it. "We live close by. I'll explain to Grandfather. Best if I prepare him." It would be unwise to confront him at once with this youth looking like a scorched Guy Fawkes rescued from a bonfire. "Follow after us, not too close. I'll explain to him as we go." She was not sure what she could explain at this stage, but she would think of something.

"I look a sight—" he faltered.

"Never mind." She could not say he didn't.

Grandfather had just begun to peer round for her. "Ah, there you are. Dropped a glove, I suppose?"

She let him suppose. "I'm sorry," she said meekly.

Farewells were said. The old gentlemen doffed their hats to her and she bobbed respectfully as she had been taught. Grandfather began to tell her of a wild rumour that the fire had been started by the Dutch. When she could get a word in, she started urgently: "Hugh Falconer—"

"That youth who hangs round our stall?" His face set instantly in disapproval.

"He's been helping to fight the fire. He's been out all night. I think perhaps his master's house is burnt – he can't go back there anyhow. He's been in the thick of it. He can tell us what's really happened." Better to be persuasive than pleading, she decided swiftly. And this appeal to the old man's curiosity worked. He looked back and let out a shocked exclamation which she feared might spell disaster. She said hurriedly: "You see the state he's in? Could we give him a chance to wash – and maybe a bite of dinner—"

"I don't know—" Grandfather became instinctively defensive.

"We've just had a sermon on Christian charity," she reminded him. It was the only thing about the sermon that she could remember.

"Very well, my dear."

He beckoned. Hugh quickened his pace to catch up with them. The old man unbent. He was not unkind by nature. "You must eat dinner with us, my boy." He knitted his shaggy eyebrows. "Perhaps we can find you a change of clothing—" Sarah stifled a smile, wondering what Hugh would look like in a clean shirt cut to her grandfather's measurements. But Hugh thanked him and said he had clean linen in his bundle.

He explained awkwardly why he was carrying the bundle. There had been a difference of opinion with his employer. Mr Biddulph had turned him out of the house the previous evening. The shaggy eyebrows shot up, but for once, to Sarah's relief, Grandfather made no comment.

They reached the house. Boy rushed barking from the yard with a welcome of such unaffected delight that Hugh's stock went up immediately. Mary paused in her cooking to provide a bowl of warm water, Fanny fetched a towel and he retired to clean himself up. Only then did Grandfather murmur, with a shake of the head, "I fear he is a wild one."

"We may find there's a good explanation," said Sarah.

And they did. By the time Hugh had told his story, over the sirloin of beef and the plum tart, even Mr Calamy had revised his opinion. "I perceive you are a lad of spirit," he said.

In any case there could have been no question of Hugh's

returning to the Biddulphs. An excited Fanny, coming in to clear the dishes, brought the latest news that had reached the kitchen. The fire was still burning fiercely. The first houses on the bridge had caught, but the wind was now driving the flames northwards from the river. They had swept up Fish Street Hill towards the heart of the City. The Star was burnt out, and St Magnus's church, all the houses thereabouts—

"Your Mr and Mrs Biddulph!" cried Sarah. "And the kind maid who brought you out your things!"

Hugh reassured her. He described what it had been like – the deafening noise, the frantic rushing to and fro. Except for the baker's maid-servant, trapped when the fire first broke out, few people could have been caught unawares. Mrs Biddulph, certainly, would have had her household up and active, saving all the possessions they could.

Even Grandfather, who had known some disastrous blazes in his long life, could remember nothing like this. "I'm minded to go and see it for myself," he announced.

Sarah cried out in dismay. Hugh advised against it. With the stifling smoke and the crowds and the trampling horses there was too much risk for a man of his age.

"I'm not a fool," said Grandfather tersely. "I'd already bespoken a waterman for this afternoon. But we'll go downstream instead of up."

# 7

The river would have been crowded with craft anyhow on such a fine September Sunday afternoon. Today it was as well that Grandfather had already engaged the services of his favourite boatman, Adam Kirby, who was waiting at Puddle Wharf in the little hoy he kept for small parties because he could navigate it alone with a pair of oars. There was ample room for Hugh as well, and the spaniel also embarked.

All the way down to the bridge the river was dotted with lighters and wherries transporting fugitives and their chattels to safety. The houses built along the northern end of the bridge were burning. Much of Thames Street, along which Hugh had walked only a few hours before, was now on fire. But the wind had veered. The advance of the flames along the riverside seemed to be slowing down. The conflagration was wheeling away and roaring into the heart of the City.

Conspicuous among the humbler craft was the royal barge, which came surging grandly past them on its way back to Whitehall. The tall figure of the King was unmistakable as he stood talking with his brother, pointing excitedly towards the bank.

"Seeing for themselves – at a safe distance," said Grandfather tartly. Though he was thankful enough that Cromwell and his crew were gone, Sarah was sometimes alarmed by his outspoken comments on the royal pair and the far from respectable lives they were known to lead.

Adam Kirby however came to their defence. "Both His

Majesty and the Duke have been ashore – and active enough, judging by what I hear. The King's sent his Guards marching into the City to help and the Duke's ordering some of his sailors up from the dockyards. The Lord Mayor's not a bit of good," he went on disgustedly. "First he makes light of it, then he's seized with panic. Flapping about like an old hen!"

"I know – I saw him last night," said Hugh.

Even here in midstream the normal freshness of the air had changed to something more like the blast from an oven-door. Flakes of wood-ash whirled about them, glowing suddenly red in the breeze, then settling as grey fragments on their clothes. Sarah saw with dismay the smuts on her clean dress. She wondered if poor Hugh had another shirt in his bundle.

Kirby pointed out landmarks as they passed. Fishmongers Hall, near the westward limit of the devastation so far, the landing-stage at Old Swan Stairs, the burnt-out warehouses of the Steelyard . . . As they neared the bridge Hugh chimed in: "Fish Street's *gone*! And St Magnus – I can make out the walls, but the roof's fallen in—"

Kirby gave Grandfather a questioning look. "You won't want to go further, Mr Calamy?"

Sarah knew what the answer would be. Grandfather never liked shooting the arches under the bridge. At many stages of the tide it was a notorious danger-spot, claiming dozens of lives every year. The arches, already narrow enough, were made even narrower by the broad flat bases on which they rested, thrusting out into the stream like giant shoes of masonry. When current clashed with incoming tide the water piled up and only a skilled boatman like Kirby cared to make the passage.

"I go by the old saying," said Grandfather. " 'London Bridge was made for wise men to go over and fools to go

44

under.' " Grandfather always liked to have a quotation to support him. Normally, if he wished to go down-river to Greenwich or Shadwell, he did as many sensible people were not ashamed to do – he stepped ashore at Old Swan Stairs and walked the short distance until he could embark again at the first landing-stage below the bridge. Today this was obviously impracticable.

"There is no reason to," said the waterman. "With the wind blowing the other way there's little to be seen."

He bent to his oars, swung the head of the boat round, and started the return journey. He was clearly not sorry to do so. Added to the normal hazards there were houses burning on the bridge and the extra risk of debris falling into the river.

On the way back he drew closer into the bank to give them a better view of what was happening. Whatever the King and the Duke of York were trying to organize to halt the fire, Sarah could see nothing but panic in this area. It was every family for itself. Boats bunched round every landing-stage and bumped into every patch of empty water beneath an overhanging upper storey. No one was trying to fight the flames. When a man saw that his own home was threatened he thought only of saving whatever personal possessions he could and escaping to the Southwark shore.

Nothing was so heavy that they would not try to get it hoisted into one of the overloaded lighters standing alongside. Enormous court cupboards, high-backed settles, gate-legged tables clapping on their hinges, dismantled four-posters with their hangings and mountainous featherbeds, everything must somehow be got away. Sarah's quick sympathy was caught by a child's high-chair with twisty oak legs like barley sugar. As a lover of music herself she held her breath while an exquisitely gilded pair of virginals was safely handed down into one of the lighters.

45

What most touched her was the distraction of the terrified pigeons. They whirled overhead, perching briefly on roofs and ledges until the heat sent them wheeling off again over the river. Always they came back. Always the flames drove them off again.

"Poor things!" she cried.

"Poor fools," said Hugh. "They can't see how useless it is."

"They don't know where else to go. This is where they nest."

"They can't reason. They're only birds."

That made her furious. "But of course! You're a *farmer*. With no feeling for dumb creatures—"

He turned on her, his face red as the fire. "And how many nights have *you* shivered on a hillside, helping a ewe to bear her lamb?"

She had no answer. She looked away, the prickle in her eyes not due to smoke. She felt he was still glowering at her, but she heard his voice again, quite altered in tone.

"Mr Kirby! Could we pull in under that house? You see the woman? With the child?"

The waterman grasped the situation at once. "Ay, leave it to me, lad. Steady! If you'll put out a hand to her—"

Sarah could only clutch the side of the boat, praying it would not capsize. Then she realized that Hugh was speaking to her, calmly as if there had been no sharp words between them. "If I pass the little boy to you—"

"Oh, be careful, Hugh!"

She stretched out her arms. The small human bundle swung lightly inboard, Hugh stooped and placed it securely in her grasp. The boat rocked alarmingly, but she was at once absorbed in comforting the infant. She was hardly aware of Hugh, a shadow between her and the sky, legs braced, one foot on the thwart, the other on the footing of

46

the wall, hand out-thrust to the young mother. Grandfather was exclaiming anxiously.

The boat tilted and bucked under the young woman's weight as she stepped awkwardly aboard. Not for the first time in her life Sarah wished devoutly that she could swim as boys could – but what chance had a modest female to learn the art or practise it afterwards, if she lived in a crowded city?

The mother sat down heavily and then reached out for her child, stammering her gratitude.

"They went without us, the others! They had my father, sick and helpless, but I had to go back for my child! They were crossing to Bankside—"

"Then you will soon be reunited, madam," said Grandfather, recovering from his own agitation. He nodded grandly to Kirby, who was already pulling thankfully back into midstream. When they had deposited the fugitives safely on the Surrey bank Grandfather declared that he had had quite enough excitement for one day, so Kirby conveyed them without further incident to Puddle Dock.

Over supper they discussed the situation. Already vast damage must have been done. How much, it was impossible to say. They had seen acres of smouldering devastation along the waterfront. They could only guess how far it had spread into the City. Where would it end?

"*Can* it have been a Dutch plot?" asked Sarah. "Or the French?"

Grandfather dismissed such rumours. "Ignorant people always look round for a scapegoat. They will blame anyone they fear or dislike – foreigners, Jews, Papists – they never think to blame themselves."

The Londoners had been warned often enough. They clung obstinately to their tumble-down old buildings, though timber and thatch made them positive death-traps. Space

47

was money. No one would give up an inch to widen a street. Rather they built out overhanging upper storeys until they almost met their neighbours opposite.

"There will be many homeless after today," he said in a sombre tone, "and many without work." He looked across the table at Hugh. "What will you do, young man?"

"Surely," said Sarah quickly, "he can stay here tonight?"

"Tonight, yes. But after?" The old man's gaze remained fixed on Hugh. "You cannot go back to your Mr Biddulph."

"I wouldn't anyhow. And his house will have gone."

"After what passed between you yesterday I fancy you may be hard put to it to find other employment in the City."

Hugh nodded grimly. "If Mr Biddulph has his way I'll never find work in London again!"

"You have a family though? In the country?"

"Ay. Herefordshire."

"That's a long way. All the same—"

"My dad's done all he can for me. There's my brothers and sisters to think of. I've vowed, I'll never go back with my tail between my legs."

"Have you any choice?"

Sarah listened miserably, not daring to butt in. She knew better than to ask Grandfather to find work for Hugh. The business was too small, her help was all he needed. He did no printing, as some of the bigger booksellers did, so Hugh's training in that field would be of no value. She could think of no suggestion to offer. But Herefordshire seemed a whole world away.

"I'll have to think," said the boy doggedly. "I have no—"

She guessed he was going to say "money" and had checked himself lest he should seem to be begging. She remembered how he had worked his way to London. But for the poor beasts it was a one-way journey to the Smithfield

48

butchers and there would be no similar casual work on the long trudge home.

"You have no what?" prompted the old man.

"I should have a paper," said Hugh quickly, "to show to the constables in the places I pass through. To prove I'm not a rogue or vagabond. I don't want to be whipped or put in some village lock-up—"

Sarah cried out. "Would they do that?"

"If they thought I might turn to begging."

"People must protect themselves," said Grandfather, "against vagrants who become a charge on the parish."

"But that's inhuman," she said.

"In the ordinary way," Hugh explained, "your master would sign a paper to show you were honest. I don't somehow fancy asking Mr Biddulph."

"No need," said Grandfather. "I shall be happy to provide that."

It occurred to Sarah that "happy" was an apt word. He was quite prepared to give Hugh shelter for tonight but less eager to do so afterwards.

Better to get the conversation away from this gloomy subject. "Shall we have some music?" she suggested.

They usually made music together on Sunday evenings and, as her grandfather often remarked, now that the Puritans no longer ran the country they were free to be as merry as they pleased, even on the Sabbath. The two maids were called in from the kitchen. Fanny had a good voice – it was a factor Grandfather had considered when engaging her – and Mary could take her part well enough. Hugh was a most welcome recruit to strengthen the male side, now that Grandfather's voice was apt to turn shrill or quavery. Sarah herself provided the accompaniment on her mother's pair of virginals, which were lifted on to the table as soon as supper was cleared.

To her relief Hugh proved to be fond of singing. He had a good ear and voice and knew most of their favourite songs. He had sung in his own home, and with the drovers, and at the printer's house off Fleet Street. "It's been like old times," he assured her when it was time to light their candles for bed. He grinned. "It was only at the Biddulphs there wasn't much singing!" His eyes, though heavy through loss of sleep the night before, were bright with the pleasure of the evening.

She herself took some while to get to sleep. Her mind was in a whirl, her curiosity and sympathy fully roused. Could nothing be done? It would be a shame if this interesting boy went back into his western hills. Would he ever see London again? More to the point, would *she* ever see *him* again? The days in Paul's Churchyard would be the duller.

Eventually she dropped off, but only to wake again after a time. Her window was bright, but not with dawn. The room glimmered pink. She jumped out of bed.

It had been a vain hope that the fire was burning itself out. It had revived. The red horizon stretched, she reckoned, from Cheapside down to the bridge. The wind was still blowing upriver, bringing hot air to her cheeks and acrid smoke into her nostrils. With such a persistent wind could not the flames get to Puddle Dock? Even here there might be danger.

She heard stealthy feet on the stairs. The maids must be creeping down from their attic. She felt a sudden need of company, someone to share her fears. She must not disturb her grandfather. Carefully she raised the latch of her door. There was no need of candles now. The staircase well was bathed in rosy light. She saw that the stealthy figure was neither Mary nor Fanny.

"I'm sorry—" Hugh's apologetic whisper was only just audible.

50

"I *was* awake."

He had been down into the yard. His room faced west and had not prepared him for the extent of the fire's progress. The yard was not much better, for at ground level the intervening mass of Baynards Castle blocked the eastward view. But the angry sky gave him a sufficient idea of the inferno that must be raging.

She cut short his whispering. "My window looks east."

"But—" He hesitated.

"Come," she said impatiently and took his hand.

She closed the door softly behind him. They tiptoed across the creaking boards. At this level they could see more than enough. The sky above the rooftops was like molten brass.

"There can't ever have been such a fire," he said huskily. "Where will it stop?"

"Lord knows." He picked out familiar landmarks. Parish churches . . . the square stone tower of the Royal Exchange with its distinctive weather-vane, the giant metal grasshopper steadily pointing the direction of this doom-laden wind . . . the stumpy tower of St Paul's . . . "If it gets as far as there—" he said, and broke off in disbelief.

"My grandfather will be out of business." She forced herself to face such a possibility.

He turned away from the view. "I mustn't stay here."

She let him out and waited till he had crossed safely to his own room. She heard the faint click of his latch behind him, then, from her grandfather's direction, a second click. With meticulous care, quite silently, she closed her door and climbed into bed.

# 8

The day dawned fine. The sky would have been unbroken blue but for the drifting veil of smoke from the east. Normally a day to rejoice over. But the maids were exclaiming, "If only it would rain!"

"It won't," Hugh assured them.

"How do you know?"

He hesitated. There were not the signs he would have looked for at home – the flying of the birds, the behaviour of the farm animals, the seeming nearness of the Black Mountains. But somehow he knew that no rain would come.

"We need the wind to go round to the west. That might bring us some. Even if it didn't it would be a help."

"How?" asked Sarah.

"It'd slow down the fire. Blow it back towards the buildings that are burnt already. But it seems set in the east."

They heard Mr Calamy coming down the stairs. Sarah looked suddenly apprehensive. Hugh guessed that she had difficulties with her grandfather, his moods and his set ways. But this morning he greeted them briskly and seemed to have become, overnight, more sympathetic to Hugh's problems. It was certainly a long way to Herefordshire, he agreed, but Hugh should have every assistance.

"I'll write you a paper to show to the constables if they ask questions. Mary will pack up some food for you. You must have money in your pocket."

"But I—"

"You can pay me back when next you come to London. *If* you come to London."

He had thought of everything. Hugh, and Sarah too, to judge from her expression, were almost overwhelmed by his decisive manner.

"But surely," she said, "we don't need to—"

He cut her short. "Once one has decided what is best to be done it is best to act quickly."

"But you've no time to write out documents for Hugh to show to constables! You said it must be business as usual today. We're late already. We should be setting out our stall."

"You must let me help," said Hugh swiftly.

They started up the hill, the dog trotting in front, the young people following respectfully at the old man's heels and suiting their pace to his.

Grateful though he was, Hugh rather resented the way Mr Calamy had taken charge of his life. The break with Mr Biddulph and now this calamitous fire had coincided most unfortunately. He knew how difficult it might be to find fresh work after such a general disaster. The Londoners would naturally look after their own folk first. None the less, he would have preferred to try his luck. It was for him to decide when he was beaten. No one else.

Sarah read his thoughts and squeezed his hand. "Don't worry. You *can't* go off like this."

"I can't stay where I'm not wanted," he whispered back. "He does not really like me."

She shook her head vehemently, but her voice lacked conviction. "He finds no fault in you – except that you're a boy. He is kind, really. But he . . . does not care for boys. And even that is only . . .' she paused, embarrassed, "because of me. But I tell him, I can look after myself."

"I'm sure you can!"

At the top of the lane they found their way blocked by a crawling procession of carts and waggons making westwards, all piled high with merchandise and household chattels, with old folk and little children wedged into any space they could find. The column was headed down Ludgate Hill to cross the bridge over the Fleet. It was only Mr Calamy's silvery locks and authoritative manner that halted the flow of fugitives just long enough for the trio to push their way through to the churchyard beyond.

There was not much sign there of business as usual.

All the leading booksellers were clustered together in voluble discussion. There was John Martin, of the Bell, with his partner James Allestry. There was Joshua Kirton, who lived over his shop on the north side. William Nott, who ran his bookbinding business at the White Horse, was there, and so was John Starkey, the notorious Anabaptist, who as usual was eloquently denouncing the government. Though Mr Calamy had only a small business he was much respected in the trade and ranked equal in this company.

Hugh waited in the background with Sarah until he should give them the word to get out the stock. They listened eagerly.

Was there a real risk of the fire reaching this far? Yesterday it had seemed unthinkable. But, with this wind still blowing, who could be sure of anything?

At least it sounded as though there was now some proper organization to fight the flames. The King and his ministers were tackling the problem energetically. The feeble Lord Mayor had been pushed aside. The Duke of York had taken supreme command, helped by a number of privy councillors and noblemen like the Earl of Manchester.

"I have no faith in these lords," Mr Starkey declared. "There is but one Lord, and He . . ."

But it was no time for religious argument and the other booksellers ignored him.

"The Middlesex magistrates have established head-quarters in Holborn," Mr Kirton announced. "At Ely Place. They've set up fire-posts at Temple Bar and Fetter Lane, Shoe Lane and . . ."

Every post was to be commanded by a Justice of the Peace. Parish constables were each to muster a hundred men and report to him. He would also have thirty soldiers and an officer under his orders.

"In the long run we shall survive by our own efforts," said Mr Martin confidently. "Every man must help his neighbour." Hugh remembered what it had been like so far. More often every man for himself.

These booksellers, however, seemed to be sensible, thoughtful men. They all knew each other. They were already bound together by their membership of the Stationers Company. They had their own hall, once a noble-man's mansion, on Ludgate Hill nearby. If the fire reached St Paul's, it was quickly agreed, they would have a better chance of saving their stock if they made a central store of it within these thick walls than if they left it in their own premises scattered in various buildings round the churchyard.

"We could mark out spaces on the floor," said Mr Martin. "There need be no confusion. Each member could make an orderly stack of his own books, labelled with his name."

Someone pointed out that even the floor space of Stationers Hall might not provide sufficient area. Someone else came forward quickly with a solution. They could use St Faith's as well. It was always regarded as the Company's church.

Hugh learnt for the first time that St Faith's was really a crypt beneath the cathedral choir, but had the status of a church in its own right. It had also a special advantage in its being underground. It would have the protection of the cathedral's massive stone walls overhead. If its doors and ventilation gratings were carefully blocked up, the place should be proof against the fire.

Mr Calamy seemed highly approving of the scheme. The tavern shed in which he stored his books overnight was built of wood. If the fire reached the churchyard it would be one of the first buildings to go up in flames. St Faith's was even handier for him than Stationers Hall.

The discussion broke up. The booksellers hurried away to begin the removal. Mr Calamy unlocked his shed and the three of them set to work. Their task was a small one compared with that of the other traders. Not only had most of them bigger stocks of books but some had their printing presses to move and supplies of paper. They had also, some of them, their homes to clear of furniture and private possessions, which they would have to load into carts, if they could hire any, and send out of the threatened area.

Mr Calamy seemed to ignore these other problems. He was confident that his own corner of Blackfriars would not be in danger. "Baynards Castle will protect us," he said. "If the fire gets that far Baynards will stop its advancing. It's a mountain of stone. Those thick walls – and the height of it . . ."

Hugh had his doubts but did not speak them. Better to save his breath for all this rushing to and fro with armfuls of heavy books. Once more, though, his memory went back to farm fires. He remembered an ancient tithe-barn. That too had been built of stone. But even a stone building had beams and rafters that the tongues of flame could lick round. Still, if Sarah was finding comfort from her grandfather's words there was no sense in destroying her peace of mind.

He was relieved to learn, from the talk between them, that the house they lived in was only rented and that the bulk of the furniture was not theirs. So, if the worst came to the worst, and Mr Calamy proved wrong in his optimism, they would not have to clear the building of its contents – a nightmare prospect, and for them an almost certain impossibility.

Even the shedful of books taxed all their energies. "It's so lucky you're here to help," Sarah panted. "I don't know how else—"

"It's nothing." But he knew that the girl and the old man would have had a hard time of it, staggering to and fro across the churchyard, negotiating those dangerously time-worn steps down into the crypt, with the excited dog weaving his way between their feet.

Mr Calamy was soon exhausted. Seeing Hugh so active he no longer attempted the heavier loads and confined himself to the specially treasured items. He had more stock than Hugh had realized. Much was never displayed on the stall. But the old man knew everything he had, from the most handsome folio volume to the slimmest pamphlet, and where to lay hands on it. There were rare items that would not be asked for in a twelvemonth, but when a customer asked for them they would be produced triumphantly, admired with many an exclamation and almost always bought.

Hugh would never entirely *like* Mr Calamy, but he had to admit he was a remarkable old man.

Sarah was watching him with the anxiety of a mother. "You have done enough, Grandfather." Soon she could say: "You must come home, now. Everything is safely stowed – thanks to Hugh. You've missed your morning draught. The maids will soon have dinner ready."

"I don't budge from here till I've seen everything made fast."

They had to wait a whole hour before the last of the booksellers had deposited his stock. The vault was full, each chalked area with its labelled stack of volumes looming in the lantern-light. At last the doors could be locked and sealed and an extra barrier of flagstones piled against them. Only then did Mr Calamy agree to go home.

While Mary and Fanny completed the dinner preparations, Hugh and Sarah took their first chance for private conversation. Would her grandfather return to the subject of Hugh's future? Would he insist on writing that document to show to suspicious constables along the road to Herefordshire?

"But I'm not *going* home – yet, anyhow," said Hugh fiercely. "He's not *my* grandfather. I'm grateful, but I'm not bound to do everything he says. If he shows me the door, I'll sleep rough. Not the first time!"

"Oh, he wouldn't! But if he does write this letter accept it gracefully. You don't have to use it. Though you might be glad of it later."

He agreed grudgingly, knowing that she was right.

By the time dinner was over, however, a more urgent problem had arisen.

Both maids looked anxious, Fanny on the verge of tears. They had heard the local talk of the way the fire was still spreading. Here too people were beginning to pack. Some had already loaded their possessions into boats and crossed to the Surrey side. Fanny vowed she would not desert her master but her parents in Southwark were afraid for her. Her brother had been over to bid her come home. She would not go without Mr Calamy's leave. Mary was calmer, but Hugh read the conflicting emotions in her face.

"We are safe enough here," said Mr Calamy crossly. And again he put forward his theory that Baynards Castle would serve as a shield and deflect the flames from advancing on Puddle Dock.

This time Hugh could not check himself from intervening. "But you've agreed, sir, it's quite possible that by tomorrow the fire may have got as far as St Paul's. What would prevent its spreading down the hill from there – getting *round* Baynards? I was thinking—"

"You think too much. *I* will do whatever thinking is necessary. But for the present, after this morning, I can rack my brain no more. So much to consider, so much to decide—"

He clambered wearily upstairs to get some rest. Sarah followed the maids into the kitchen, sympathizing, sharing their anxieties, trying to hide her own. Hugh felt useless in this agitated household to which he did not belong. He might be of service to someone elsewhere. At least he would discover what was going on. He set off, walking eastwards, against the stream of fugitives.

The evacuation was becoming a rout, worsening hour by hour. Men had come in from the surrounding countryside, any man who could get hold of a horse and cart. Like the boatmen along the waterfront they were reaping a rich harvest from the desperate householders. Thieves and tricksters too seemed to have emerged from the underworld like insects from the woodwork. Their ingratiating smiles and helpful hands were the biggest immediate danger. Whatever they laid hold of was apt to vanish with them and not be seen again.

He saw one gang, bolder than the rest, who made no pretence of helping but simply started looting a shop that was being cleared. The owners resisted desperately. Hugh was pushing his way forward to help them when there came a clatter and jingle of approaching horsemen and a warning shout, "The Duke!" The looters dropped their booty and vanished into the crowd. The King's brother and his bodyguard were riding up and down through the City to prevent just this sort of incident.

The Duke reined in and called to a seaman who stepped forward and saluted him. "How are things going, bo'sun?"

"Doing what we can, your grace. The folks don't like us pulling their houses down—"

"Who would? They must see, they'll burn anyhow. But if we demolish them first we'll have a fire-break – it's the surest way to save other property."

"Beg pardon, your grace – if only we were allowed to use gunpowder! It's speed that matters—"

"True enough. I must consider . . . Meantime, do your best."

"Ay, ay, sir. We will. Depend on that."

The Duke and his party clattered off again.

As before, Hugh found that his knowledge of horses was his most welcome asset. He met a little convoy of laden waggons forced to a standstill by the press of people. He helped to extricate them and escorted them as far as Cripplegate on the northern boundary of the City. It was alarming to find that the fire had spread thus far.

At Cripplegate he found King Charles himself, dismounted, his swarthy face black with soot, wielding shovel and bucket as energetically as anyone. He had a pouch slung over his shoulder, clinking with guineas. Hugh caught the golden gleam as he pulled out a coin to reward a party of demolition men. Like his brother he saw fire-breaks as the best answer.

Hugh was dead-beat when he dragged himself back to Puddle Dock. He was eagerly questioned for news but it was difficult to give a clear picture. One thing was certain: the flames were still spreading remorselessly and this continuing east wind was to blame.

"The fire's scarcely burning back at all," he said. "It seems it's barely reached Billingsgate yet, though that's only a stone's throw from where it started in Pudding Lane. But of course Billingsgate is down-river and the wind's the other way."

"This way," said Sarah gloomily.

Mary rushed in from the kitchen. "Beg pardon, Mr Calamy, sir . . ."

"What is it now?"

"Baynards is all alight, sir! We can see flames coming out o' the windows!"

# 9

A crowd had gathered. Puddle Dock offered a clear view of the Norman fortress, without obstructing houses, from its topmost battlements down to the landing-stairs in the river lapping its base.

Night had come, but not darkness. The smoke pall which had blotted out the sun all day now acted as a reflector for the burning buildings and the whole scene was bathed in a hellish glow. The flint walls of Baynards might not burn but the interior of the castle was well ablaze. The narrow windows gave it the look of a gigantic brazier filled with red-hot coals.

Fanny was sobbing. "God help us all!"

In an awed tone Mr Calamy said, "Richard Crookback was lodged in that tower when his followers came and offered him the crown of England." He seemed stunned that such an historic landmark should be swept away. At this critical moment it was less important to Hugh. But Sarah's grandfather drew comfort from such remarks. If he could find a link with some tag of book-learning he felt more in control of the situation.

"What will become of us, sir?" Mary asked him.

"We'll know better in the morning. If the castle is burnt out it may provide the barrier we need. But if our house is threatened we must abandon it."

"Where can we go?" said Sarah.

"My good friend Mr Bolton will take us in."

"But he lives right down at Shadwell!"

"Adam Kirby will transport us."

"Are you sure Mr Bolton will take us in?"

"He can hardly refuse. He has room and to spare. We've been friends for many years. I've found countless rare books for him. Do not worry, my dear. We shall see how things stand in the morning."

He waddled back to the house. The maids followed. Sarah and Hugh stayed, staring with fascination across the dock. The flames were reflected in the water, frenziedly dancing chains of red and gold. He said, hesitantly, "It's not for me to say—"

"Say it!"

"Your grandfather should not leave everything until tomorrow—"

"He won't be hurried, not by anyone."

"But by the fire, maybe. Fire doesn't wait for anyone, even your grandfather. I've seen so many of these poor people who've put things off till it was too late—"

"Oh, Hugh—" Her face looked drawn in the flickering light. "What ought he to be doing?"

"He should send word to the waterman. Mr Kirby will have other calls upon him. It's been like that with the carters and waggoners." He described the chaos in the streets that afternoon. "All along the river there'll be people frantic to get across to Southwark. And if your grandfather has a longer journey in mind he'd best send to Mr Kirby tonight and strike a bargain—"

"But he's still hoping against hope we shan't have to go. You heard him."

"I did," said Hugh gloomily.

"I don't know what *I* can do." Then she corrected herself. "Perhaps a quiet word with Mary and Fanny. To get everything ready tonight – in case. Bale up the linen and blankets, pack his precious bottles of wine in lots of straw, do whatever can be done without his noticing. And if we don't have to go, everything can be put back and he'll never know. I'll sort out my own clothes—"

"My packing will be simple," he said with a laugh.

She looked at him keenly. "You will come with us – if we have to go? You must."

"I'll see you all safely landed at Shadwell. I reckon you'll need a hand. After that . . ." He shrugged.

There had still been no discussion of his future. After the help he had already given, Mr Calamy could hardly refuse his services until this emergency was over.

"You must stay with us," she said emphatically.

"This Mr Bolton won't want *me*. Once you're there, I must fend for myself."

"You're as stubborn as Grandfather!"

She hurried back to the house. He stayed, grimly watching the fire and talking to the other onlookers.

Mary and Fanny promised to make discreet preparations for departure in the morning if it became necessary. She went up to her room. Boy trotted softly after her, uneasy with so much tension in the air. "*You* shan't be left behind," she assured him in a whisper. She folded clothes and laid them in her chest. Many, threadbare or outgrown, could be abandoned. There were not many recent acquisitions. It did not occur to her grandfather that a girl hankered after a new dress for Easter, unless it was obviously essential. She hesitated to ask. So the chest would hold everything, dresses and petticoats, shifts and other under-linen, winter cloak and hood, slippers and stockings and pattens for muddy walking. Into odd corners went her few private treasures, her mother's rings, a miniature, her prayerbook.

She went downstairs again. Grandfather was sitting at the table. Neat little stacks of gold coins glinted in the candle-

63

light. He looked up, startled. "Close the door," he said. "That boy – Hugh – he is out?"

"Yes. But you need not be afraid." There was the slightest edge to her voice. "He's as honest as the day."

"I am sure he is. But it's wrong – at a time like this – to put temptation in anyone's way."

She was glad to see the open cash-box. It showed that, for all his display of confidence, even he was preparing for the worst.

The dog gave her an excuse to slip out again. She found Hugh where she had left him. "You're quiet," she said. "What are you thinking about?"

"Tomorrow."

She wondered if his thoughts were like her own. Would it mean as much to him if, after tonight, he never saw them again?

"Tomorrow. Yes. We had better try to get some sleep." She called Boy and they walked slowly back along the wharf.

At dawn she saw from her window that Baynards still stood, its walls blackened, its interior gutted, its windows like empty eye-sockets staring blindly through the haze that drifted from the smouldering ashes within. At least the flames had made no further progress towards Puddle Dock.

"As I hoped," said Grandfather in triumph, "all that masonry has served us as a shield!"

"Praise the Lord!" cried Mary. "We may not have to go."

She spoke too soon. Within the hour they heard the jangle of a bell and the stentorian voice of the public crier, announcing as he came down the lane: "By order of His Royal Highness the Duke of York! All people to clear their goods and vacate their houses immediately! God save the King!"

His Grace, it seemed, had taken over personal command

in Blackfriars. He was determined to make a thoroughly effective fire-break.

Blackfriars was doomed anyhow. Further from the water-front the first flames had reached Paul's Churchyard. Almost every minute brought more and more alarming news. The cathedral itself had caught, the roof was burning, its molten lead was cascading down in a boiling stream. The fire would in time creep down the hill and reach Puddle Dock that way.

The obvious line for a fire-break was the course of the Fleet, running down from the bridge at Ludgate to where it entered the Thames. But the Fleet was only a narrow stream, too narrow to form an adequate barrier, and both its banks were cluttered with wooden sheds and workshops, and even privies built out above the water. All these must be ruthlessly swept away. Whatever would burn, timber or thatch, must be thrown into the stream and washed down into the river.

Even then, the belt of cleared ground would not be wide enough to prevent sparks from being blown across to spread the fire into Fleet Street. So the thorough-going Duke had ordered the demolition of all houses on the Blackfriars side. So far, Hugh pointed out, every attempt at a fire-break elsewhere had failed through doing too little too late. He tried to make Grandfather see this, but the old man turned away in angry irritation.

"Sarah," he said, "run and find Adam Kirby. Tell him I want to be taken down to Shadwell. The five of us and all our belongings. In his bigger boat, the wherry. Twelve o'clock, say. I refuse to be hurried."

Hugh went down to the wharf with her. Kirby was not to be seen, but she got news of him from a family she knew, who were clustered patiently beside a small mountain of their chattels. They had themselves engaged him to take them up to Westminster. He had just left with a boatload bound for Chelsea.

"But he won't forget us," an old grandmother kept repeating cheerfully. "Mr Kirby is a man of his word." Unfortunately it sounded as though the reliable Kirby had already given his word to a great number of other people.

Hugh was looking round anxiously. The crowd on the wharf was swelling as more and more houses were hastily vacated. Boats kept edging into the wharf to be quickly filled with would-be passengers, begging to be taken up or down the river or even just across to the Surrey bank. When poor Kirby arrived back with his empty wherry he had to face a shock himself – the news of the Duke's order and the realization that he too now had a home to clear and a family of his own to take to safety.

Sarah managed to catch his eye and stammer Grandfather's optimistic message. He managed wonderfully to maintain his calm. "My respects to Mr Calamy! Give him my word, I won't fail him. But I have a day's work ahead of me – and now, somehow, I must think of my own folk."

"Of course. You must look after your own."

"But I will get Mr Calamy to Shadwell by tonight." He grinned apologetically. "And that, Lord forgive me, is the last promise I can make to anyone this day."

She thanked him warmly. They turned for home, content with his pledge and hoping that Grandfather would be equally satisfied.

"You could do no more," Hugh assured her. "I wondered at first if we should try to hire another boatman, but when I saw what it was like—"

"It would have been hopeless."

The demolition men had begun work. On both banks of the Fleet they were tearing down the flimsy thatch and timber outbuildings. Now they were starting on the houses, wrenching out doors and window-frames, stairways and pan-elling, anything combustible, almost before the lamenting occupants had vacated their homes. Fire-hooks laid their iron claws upon the roofs and heaved. Rafters and beams came crashing down, age-old dust mingling with the omin-ously advancing smoke.

The Duke was now there in person, frowning down from his saddle, rapping out orders as though he were on the quarterdeck in a storm at sea. It would have been fine, thought Sarah, if it had been a storm at sea. The Navy swore by the Duke as Lord High Admiral, but at this moment something more like the King's warm-hearted sympathy would have gone down better in Blackfriars. Many years later she was to think back to this day, the only time she had ever seen James Stuart close at hand. She would under-stand then why, having become king, he could so soon have lost the crown Charles had managed to keep.

"This is all too slow," the Duke was shouting. "Hasn't the gunpowder arrived from Deptford? It's the only way."

Grandfather was almost incoherent with dismay. Hugh kept his head. It was well, thought Sarah, that someone could. He was even, somehow, managing to handle her grandfather.

"I think, sir," he suggested quietly, "it would be wise to start carrying your goods down to the wharf. It may be hours before Mr Kirby can take us off, but they will be safer on the open dockside. We cannot leave them in the house any longer. And if they start using gunpowder—"

There was no need to finish the sentence even for Grand-father. "They are really going to do that?" he said feebly.

"I'm afraid so," said Hugh gravely. Sarah thought to herself, He can't wait for them to start – he's sure it's the best thing, but he doesn't want to upset Grandfather any more. Aloud she said: "I saw a boat pull in just now, full

67

of sailors. They'd brought a lot of kegs – they were unloading them on the wharf—"

"And it won't be rum," said Hugh.

Mary had set out cold beef, cheese, a loaf, and mugs of small beer. They ate standing, afraid now to delay longer. All these chests and bundles must be carried down to the waterfront. Fanny had found two muscular young men from the tavern and enlisted their help with the heavier loads.

A distant explosion indicated that the naval party had started its work. "Hark at that!" said Hugh. There was a second explosion, then, at intervals of only a few seconds, three more. "They don't waste time."

One of the young men seemed knowledgeable. "They put a keg of powder in each house, and lay a train from one to another . . ."

A seaman loomed in the doorway. "Best be getting out, sir. We're doing this row next."

They abandoned their meal. Hugh seemed to take charge. "Mr Calamy wants everything taken to the wharf and stacked. Where Adam Kirby moors his boats."

They all set to work. Sarah seized a bale of bed-linen, Grandfather hugged his cash-box, Hugh carried her precious pair of virginals, the maids loaded themselves with the pewter and glass they had already packed. Even with their two helpers it took them a number of journeys before everything was gathered in a dump on the wharf. They were just one family group among many, some tearful, some hysterical, some simply dazed.

Sarah prompted her grandfather and he paid off the helpers. It was just a question now of waiting on the quay until Kirby had fulfilled his other promises. Most likely he would leave them to the last, when all his shorter trips had been made. His own house was being cleared by his capable wife and daughters. We may be here for hours yet, thought Sarah philosophically, but Adam Kirby won't fail us. The open wharf would be safe. If the fire got dangerously near they would have to get down into the water and hold on to the mooring rings.

"Where is my stick?" Grandfather demanded abruptly. "I put it down somewhere, when I needed both hands. It's too old a friend to be left behind."

He began to shuffle purposefully along the quay. Sarah ran after him. Hugh had strolled off to watch the seamen at work. "Grandfather!" she called. "Let me go—"

He turned and waved her back impatiently. "You won't know where to look. Stay here with the dog and keep an eye on everything."

She dare not disobey. She went back. Raising her eyes she saw the huge mass of the cathedral with flames streaming through gashes in its roof. Now that so many of the intervening buildings had been demolished there was a clearer view. Usually the gunpowder blew out the walls and left the timber frame of each house standing like a skeleton, which then slowly collapsed upon the ruins.

Hugh was back at her side. "It's wonderful how the sailors set about it," he began admiringly. Then his tone changed. "Where's your grandfather?"

"He'd left his stick in the house—"

He cried out in alarm. "They're getting to your end of the lane—"

She was already running back. She ignored his shout. She heard his racing footsteps on the cobbles behind her. She strained her eyes for a glimpse of her grandfather coming back.

A seaman barred her way. "I just want—" she pleaded despairingly.

"Too late now, my dear! All this lot is going up!"

She could not break the hold of that kindly bear-like arm.

69

The man saw Hugh, swore at him roundly, and thrust out his other arm, but Hugh swerved out of his reach and rushed on.

Sarah screamed. She saw him vanish into the yawning doorway of the house. In the same instant, from somewhere near at hand, came the first thunderous explosion.

# 10

Hugh heard that explosion a mere moment after he had found Mr Calamy. The old man had recovered his stick and was waving it in triumph, chanting some Latin tag.

He seemed not to have noticed what had instantly caught Hugh's eye – the sinister-looking little keg, the tell-tale peppering of gunpowder leading to it through one doorway and out again through another towards the next house.

"Quick, sir!" Hugh had just time to shout before the first shattering explosion came from higher up the lane. The house rocked. The window blew in, showering them with splintered glass. There was a rush, a gale almost, of acrid fumes.

It was no moment for courtesies. He grabbed Mr Calamy's arm and hustled him towards the door. There was a second detonation, even louder, even nearer. Again the house shuddered, again a bitter yellowish cloud billowed in, half choking them. Looking back, as he helped the stumbling bookseller, he saw through the haze the devilish glitter of the powder train as it came alive and began its snake-like course across the floor.

It was providential that Mr Calamy tripped on the doorstep and shot sprawling into the roadway. And that Hugh went flying out on top of him, shielding him from the hail of debris that rained down on them. Had they been standing upright when the keg exploded they might have been killed. Even Sarah, much further away, was blown off her feet.

Hugh jumped up, anxious only to get Mr Calamy out of

71

range. The house they had just left was outlined against the dirty-white sky, roof gone, lath and plaster scattered in all directions. Only the basic structure of beams remained upright, its framework of vertical and horizontal and slanting lines like some diagram in geometry. Then it shuddered, and with the absurd dignity of a drunken man it folded and slowly collapsed on the layer of rubble beneath. One by one the remaining houses in the row followed suit as the spluttering powder train raced in and out of their doors. By the time Hugh had restored the breathless old man to his granddaughter the whole street behind them was flat.

They staggered thankfully back to the comparative safety of the wharf.

Blackfriars was now a picture of utter desolation. The demolitions gave them a clearer view. Behind Baynards – now a mere skull of pale, soot-streaked masonry – the warehouses of Thames Street were still burning fitfully. To the left, up the hill, the whole area round St Paul's was an inferno. The booksellers had been well justified in their precautions yesterday.

The wharf was still crowded with fugitives waiting for boats to take them off. Earlier in the day many had escaped by the bridge across the Fleet at Ludgate. But it had been hard to find carts to carry their furniture and most of them turned to their normal mode of transport, a boat from Puddle Dock. Now the escape-route via Fleet Street was blocked. Blackfriars had become an island, with fire on two sides, the Thames on another, and the Fleet on the fourth. One could, of course, scramble across that shallow stinking stream – easier now that it was choked with the debris of the demolished sheds – but it would have meant going almost empty-handed. Grandfather was not the only one who clung to such few possessions as remained to him.

"Adam Kirby will not fail us," he said.

72

It was getting late. And they were all hungry. They had been forced to abandon their midday snap half-eaten and even the reliable Mary had never foreseen that suppertime would find them still waiting on the riverfront. They got reassuring glimpses of Mr Kirby at intervals, when he returned from one trip and filled up with another boatload. With a wave and a grin he would show that they were not forgotten, but, as they had expected, their turn would not come until the end.

Mr Kirby's craft today was a broad-beamed wherry, a double-sculler, the other pair of oars being handled by his senior apprentice, a powerful-looking twenty-year-old. It was a roomy craft, and though it could not take a houseful of bulky furniture – that was a job for the lightermen – it was remarkable what they could load into it.

"They look dead-beat," said Sarah, full of sympathy.

"They'll keep going till the last job is done," Hugh reassured her. He remembered the long days of harvest and haymaking. "Wonderful what you can do when you're working against the weather or the failing of the light."

Light at least would not be the problem. A red glow lit up the whole scene, made brighter by the reflection from the river.

At last the waiting crowd had dwindled to a few dozen weary and almost silent people. Nobody else, they found, was waiting for Adam Kirby. They should be the next, and the last. And soon there he was, shipping his oars and stepping on to the wharf only a little less smartly than usual.

Mr Calamy brushed aside his apologies. "You are very good. I knew I could depend on you."

"I wouldn't have chosen this stage of the tide," said the waterman frankly. "But there was no choice. Never fear, sir, we shall be safe enough. I've made this passage so many times."

It was the bridge, of course, thought Hugh. The old man would not relish the shooting of those narrow arches when the tide was coming in like this. But there could be no question of landing and then embarking again while the whole waterfront of the City was still in the grip of the fire. And the landing-places on the Surrey side were much fewer and further apart. After the day he had been through Mr Calamy was in no state for further exertion.

Hugh himself was tired enough. At any normal time he would have looked forward to the pleasurable excitement of shooting the bridge against the incoming tide. He had never done so. Indeed, since coming to London, he had not had much occasion to be on the river at all. At this moment, though, he was in no mood for the experience. After a day so full of excitements and anxieties he longed for food, drink and a long sleep in any corner Mr Bolton could provide.

No time was wasted in loading the boat. Everyone but Mr Calamy tried to help. Sarah lifted what she could and attempted to lift what she could not, until Mr Kirby shouted tactfully, "What would help most, Miss Sarah – if you could hold on to your little dog—" Boy was rushing round them frenziedly, getting in everybody's way. Sarah obeyed meekly and took her seat beside her grandfather. Mr Kirby waved the others to their places. He preferred, with the help of the big apprentice, to arrange the loading himself and ensure a proper balance.

"That's it, then," he cried at last. They pushed out into the glimmering stream. Half a mile away the bridge stretched its long line of arches from bank to bank.

The ancient structure looked, in the firelight playing on it, surprisingly undamaged. Only the houses at its northern end had suffered seriously. Overhanging parts of them had tumbled into the river or, Mr Kirby reported, into the roadway behind. That, he said, was completely blocked, so that neither coach nor cart could pass over into Southwark. In the centre of the bridge, where the gap came in the double row of shops and dwellings, the flames had halted. Sparks had blown across on the wind, and fires had started in a couple of houses, but they had been quickly put out.

Hugh was crouched in the bows, twisted round to study the bridge as it loomed ever nearer. Mr Kirby and his assistant pulled manfully on their oars, Mr Kirby glancing occasionally over his shoulder and grunting some curt instruction as he headed for the archway he meant to pass through. When Hugh looked back down the boat he had only glimpses of the others, half-hidden by the piles of objects stowed between them. He could make out Grandfather, nursing his brass-bound cash-box, and Sarah bent forward to soothe the unseen spaniel at her feet. The maids were huddled in the stern.

The chosen archway rose ahead, a yawning tunnel, black in contrast with the dancing firelight which showed up every detail of the masonry outside. The darkness under the arch was relieved only by the luminous white flurry of foam where the river current piled up and battled with the incoming tide.

Hugh straightened himself on his seat, gripping both sides of the boat. In a few moments this nerve-racking manoeuvre would be safely accomplished and the tension relaxed. Both the bridge and the burning city would be behind them, and they would have a clear course down to Shadwell.

Boy chose that moment to resume his freedom. He sprang forward with a bark of excitement. Hugh heard Sarah desperately calling him back, heard his paws scrabbling up the mound of baggage in front of him. "Boy!" she implored him. Against the curved background of pink sky outside the arch Hugh could see a silhouetted figure rise up, swaying.

He heard Grandfather's urgent command: "Sit *down*, girl!" Mr Kirby's voice rang out, adding his warning.

Both men were too late. The silhouette was gone. In the roar of the waters Hugh only dimly heard the splash as Sarah went overboard.

# 11

Instinctively Hugh cried out to the waterman, but the man needed no telling. The wherry reared like a horse as it met the tumble of the rapids. It was barely controllable and needed all Kirby's skill to prevent its being swamped.

Hugh leapt to his feet, kicked off his shoes, and jumped over the side. He dared not dive, not knowing the depth. His feet just touched bottom before he shot up again. Deep enough for drowning.

For himself he had no fear. He had learnt his swimming in the fast rivers of the Welsh Marches, with their swirling cataracts and bottomless salmon pools. But Sarah – could she swim a stroke?

The boat shot past him. He ducked under an oar but caught a glancing blow that for a moment stunned him. No other head bobbed above the surface. Underwater, his arms and legs encountered no other body. He took a long breath and plunged down, groping desperately. To no purpose. In this turbulent water nothing would stay submerged in one spot.

He fought his way out of the dark archway, fighting the relentless tide. The boat had passed through safely, Kirby was striving now to swing it round. He prayed that he might see them hauling Sarah over its side, but their shouts told him at once that they had seen no sign of her.

"There's naught you can do for the poor lass!" Kirby's brawny arm stretched out to help him.

"We can't just leave her here!" Hugh's voice choked with horror.

The waterman got a grip on his shoulder. "She's not here, God help her. She'll have been swept on downstream by now. Or carried back by the tide. It's hopeless, any road. We must think of Mr Calamy, poor soul. We must get him safe to his friends—"

Hugh was in no position to argue. This man knew the river, its hazards and uncertainties. Upstream, downstream, the girl might be anywhere by now, a lifeless body somewhere beneath the surface. Search was impossible. He allowed himself to be pulled dripping into the boat.

"Keep an eye out for her as we go," said Kirby.

"I will," Hugh gasped. He scrambled to the empty place on the thwart beside Mr Calamy.

The old man was still dazed by what had happened. "God have mercy on her, poor child," he muttered again and again. "All in a moment! The Lord giveth and the Lord taketh away."

The Lord had not taken the cause of the tragedy, thought Hugh grimly. Boy crouched whimpering between his feet, uneasy but uncomprehending of the reason for his disgrace. Poor brute. Hugh realized that his own resentment was unjust. He reached down and stroked the shaggy coat. "It wasn't your fault," he whispered. "She just – loved you too much."

The only hope, and a slender one, was that Sarah was still alive and afloat somewhere ahead of them, perhaps clinging to some piece of timber. There were always objects to be seen drifting on the surface of the river. Tonight, because of all the demolitions, it was dotted more thickly than ever with such wreckage. More than once his anxious eyes deceived him into mistaking some dim shape for a human creature gripping the floating object. He would cry

78

out, and Kirby would turn his head and alter course to investigate. Always the hope proved false.

They passed Billingsgate. The fire had reached the great fish-market at last, where Mr Biddulph had been so important a personage, and the scene of his glory was now reduced to ashes. Now, even with the wind against them, the flames were battling their way along the bank to Botolph's Wharf and the Custom House. Ahead loomed the Tower, pale white in what was now unclouded moonlight. Surely its wide moat and high walls would bar any further progress of the flames? Yet even here the sailors were clearing a broad swathe through the adjacent houses. The Duke was taking no chances. The Tower armouries held immense stocks of gunpowder. If the fire got to them much of London could be blown sky-high.

Other craft were running upriver on the tide. Kirby hailed them as they passed. But no one had sighted a girl in the water, much less pulled her out.

Hugh's heart sank, heavy as a stone. He forced himself to console poor Mr Calamy, mumbling brokenly beside him, but he could get little conviction into his tone. He had heard enough of the river and its ways while serving in the Biddulph household. The hated Pearse had gloated over his descriptions of corpses washed to and fro with the change of tides, emerging on the surface only after days of being submerged, when they were swollen and horribly distorted with putrefaction. Even when rescued alive, the footman had loved to explain, they often died from the foul water they had swallowed. "Got to remember," Pearse would say with a coarse leer, "everything goes into the river – everything!"

Hugh's stomach rose as he remembered Pearse's ghoulish pleasure in these accounts.

They passed Wapping. The river bent northwards. The

wind brought the salt tang of the sea. Houses and workshops straggled along the bank. There seemed no end to the outward spread of London. Now, said Kirby, they were nearly at Shadwell. Though it was getting late the place was still astir. People could be seen standing about, staring at the red smoke-pall hanging over the city.

Mr Bolton's house stood near the wharf, one of the most imposing residences in Shadwell, which had been a fashionable suburb fifty years ago, before the wealthier people moved out. There was ample space in it for Mr Calamy's small party and they were given a warm welcome, for the kindly Boltons had been greatly concerned for their safety at Blackfriars. Joy turned to shock and grief when they heard of Sarah's tragic fall into the river.

Hugh's impressions of that arrival were sketchy. He was soaked to the skin, famished, and still dazed by the whole experience. He was thankful to gulp down a bowl of hot stew, peel off his clinging wet clothes, and crawl into the truckle bed that was quickly made up and warmed for him. The bewildered spaniel would not leave him and he had not the heart to drive him away. Boy ended by snuggling in beside him and Hugh was glad of the companionship.

With daylight reality rushed back. It was true, then, not a nightmare. A scream from Sarah in the darkness below the bridge . . . then she was gone. It had happened.

Mr Bolton questioned him. Mr Calamy was still in deep sleep, helped by the mulled wine he had been given the night before. "You are not related to him?" asked Mr Bolton. "Did you work for him? I remember only poor Sarah at the stall."

Hugh explained how slender was his connection. His host reassured him. "There's room for you here, until you can decide upon your future."

Hugh's only plan for the future was to walk back along

80

the riverbank and see if he could pick up any news of Sarah. It was a forlorn hope, but how, at a time like this, could one think of anything else?

Mr Bolton eyed him sympathetically. "You're a sensible lad, I'm sure. If the poor girl *has* been found – one never knows – you could" – he hesitated – "identify her?"

"Of course!"

"In that case" – Mr Bolton was trying to choose his words carefully – "claim – the body. On behalf of Mr Calamy. Explain he's here. We can send . . . If we're allowed to take her. But – you understand about inquests?"

Hugh remembered *Hamlet*. "Like Ophelia?"

The reference seemed to confirm Mr Bolton in his judgment of Hugh. "Exactly," he said hurriedly. "But we have to find her first, before we think of Christian burial."

Hugh was glad to end this mournful conversation. He set out, munching his buttered hunk of bread, the dog at his heels.

But for that baleful smoke-cloud in the west it would have been just another golden morning in September. On his left the river stretched blue and innocent. On his right, beyond the thin belt of houses, the fields were alive with harvesters. At any other time he might have felt a wave of homesickness. Not today.

He must keep his eyes on the river, its mud-flats, and anything drifting seaward. There were plenty of men about, scouring the bank for beams or barrels or anything else of use. He questioned everyone he passed, heart in mouth until he had their answer. No one had seen a body. But, he reminded himself, there had been all those hours of darkness.

He passed through Wapping. There were still more people, because of the shipyards and alum-works. He could not ask everyone he saw, only hope that the word would have gone round if a girl had been pulled out of the water. Another mile brought him to Tower Wharf. It was there that a workman shouted to him. "You were calling your dog just then. 'Boy'? That his name, is it?"

"Yes. Why?"

"There was a poor wench last night. Crying out 'Boy' something piteous. And it was a dog she was after."

Other men quickly clustered round. "They'd just fished her out of the river," one explained. "Thought at first she was gone, but no, she opens her eyes and starts asking for this 'Boy'."

Hugh's mind reeled with relief. "So she's alive?"

"Right as rain. An' twice as wet," the man added humorously. "Good-looking young woman – well, girl I'd say."

"Where is she now? Where did she go?"

There was uncertainty about that. Several voices contributed scraps of information or guesswork.

She'd fallen out of a boat. She'd taken a nasty knock on the head and didn't seem at all herself. She'd been bound for Shadwell, she thought, but she'd fainted away again before she could give any further details.

"There was a couple passing with a cart," someone recalled. "Getting out quick with all their belongings. They offered to look after her. You couldn't just leave her."

"And where were *they* going?"

"They didn't know theirselves. Anywhere, they said, safe from the fire. Hampstead, maybe, or Highgate. Lord knows."

"If she's alive," Hugh said, "I'll find her wherever she is."

# 12

"So you've woke at last, my duck?"

Sarah groaned, opened her eyes, and saw a woman bending over her. A homely moon face, ugly and pockmarked but kindly. "What happened?" she stammered. "Where am I?"

Sunlight slanted through an open door. She was in some sort of hut. A row of pewter tankards hung along one wall. There was a stack of bundles and boxes, but not those which had been loaded into the boat. Nor, certainly, was she in her own bed. Only this lumpy mattress lay between her and a floor which was merely trodden earth. As her bare legs touched under the blanket she realized that she was wearing nothing but a rough shift, itchier than any she had ever known.

She sat up. A pain shot through her head. She felt a bruise, a patch of blood-matted hair. "Where am I?" she asked. "Where are my clothes?"

"They were soaked, my duck, and foul from the river. I hung them on the bushes to dry."

"But where *am* I?" She could hear a babble of many voices outside like the ceaseless murmur of Paul's Churchyard. She smelt smoke. That smell had hardly been out of her nostrils these past three days, but now it was mixed with country smells, horse sweat and trampled grass.

"We're at Moorfields," said the woman. "My husband reckoned it was the nearest open ground to make for."

Sarah knew Moorfields. She and Grandfather had walked

Boy there – it was certainly the handiest open space for Puddle Dock. Just north of the ancient city wall, a former marshland, long ago drained and made into a public pleasure-ground with curving paths and arched footbridges over ditches where yellow flags bloomed. The hut must be one of those that sold food and drink on fine summer evenings.

Hugh had said that thousands of homeless people were camping out at Moorfields . . . But where *was* Hugh? And Grandfather?

The woman asked her name. "You couldn't tell us, last night. Seems you'd just been fished out of the river, half-drowned! You couldn't just be left there. I said to my husband, 'There's room in the cart.' He wouldn't have it at first, but I got round him—"

"You were very kind—"

A man's figure blocked the doorway. "Talking now, is she? That's better." He loomed large in the tiny hut. He crouched beside her and she caught a whiff of the liquor on his breath. He showed his teeth – such as remained to him – in an amiable but sinister-looking grin. She pulled up the blanket to her chin. He questioned her keenly.

"And who's this grandfather?"

"Mr Calamy. The bookseller, he's well known—"

"Books, eh?" He sounded disappointed. "No money in *them*. And this friend you were going to?"

"Mr Bolton. He's a timber-merchant in a big way at Shadwell. They must think I'm dead!" Sarah turned appealingly to the woman. "If my clothes are dry—"

The woman started to speak but the man silenced her. "No hurry, Sukey. She's in no state to walk all that way by herself. Got a bit of paper, and pen an' ink?"

His wife looked flabbergasted by this unexpected demand. "I – I don't think so, Gabriel—"

It was an incongruous name for this man. Neither his appearance nor his manner in the least suggested an angel. He snarled at the woman. "Not much use, are you? We'll have to ask around then." He turned back to Sarah. "*You* can write?"

"Of course," said Sarah, controlling her indignation.

"Then you can write to your grandfather, once we got pen an' paper. Tell him you're safe and sound. Say you owe your life – to the bearer." He brought out the last phrase with some satisfaction. "Who rescued you at considerable danger to his own life."

Sukey let out a gasp which he quelled with a scowl. She was clearly terrified of him. Sarah herself was getting more and more uneasy.

"I can tell him the rest myself," Gabriel went on. "I'm sure your grandad and I can come to a satisfactory understanding. He should be mighty grateful to have you back."

"I'm sure he will." Sarah tried hard to control her voice, keeping out all sign of alarm. It was obvious – this man was going to hold her to ransom. Best for the moment to seem meek and innocent. "If I could have my clothes . . ." she suggested, turning to Sukey. The woman opened her mouth to answer but as usual the man spoke.

"In good time. You're best snug in bed for now."

Just then, from the distance, came the brazen peal of a handbell, and a singsong public announcement that there was to be a free distribution of bread. The man stood up. "Best get our share of anything that's going."

"Shouldn't I stay here?" Sukey enquired timidly.

"Nay, we can get double, going up separate. She'll be all right. Can't go far, a young lady like her, not in the circumstances." He laughed coarsely. Sarah hugged the blanket more tightly round her. He grinned back from the doorway. "We'll be back. We'll get that pen an' paper while

85

we're at it. The doors of these huts," he added meaningly, "are barred from the outside." He shut the door behind him and she heard the heavy bars thud into their sockets. A padlock snicked. No doubt he had picked it last night to get into the hut. It would have been child's play to a man like Gabriel.

He was so maddeningly cocksure, this scoundrel. Her fury almost drove out her fear. Somehow, she determined, she was going to escape from this place before they came back.

She ran to the door, pushed at it, flung her weight against it. It did not budge, as she had known it would not. She began to shout, she picked up one of the smaller boxes and banged it against the door. Her noise produced no response. Outside, silence had replaced the previous hubbub of voices. Everyone must have rushed off to the bread distribution. She dared not wait until some of them returned and heard her appeals for help.

There was no window to the hut, but— That reminded her. One warm evening she and Grandfather had gone to a hut like this and refreshed themselves with mugs of small beer. The man inside the hut had served them across a sort of counter which was a hinged board let down on supporting chains like a castle drawbridge. Or a shutter, Grandfather had said less romantically, but opening horizontally instead of vertically. If this hut was built like that and the counter could be let down from inside—

It was, and it did. She groped, found the bolts that locked it to the walls on either side. The board fell outwards on its supporting chains and sunshine poured in to replace the gloom. A few yards away she saw her best petticoat, the lace-edged one, draped over a gorse bush. Near it hung her dress, smock, stockings, everything.

There was nobody in sight except for the distant crowd

thronging round the waggon from which the bread was being doled out. The intervening space was dotted with tents and makeshift shelters and empty carts with horses grazing near. But in this middle distance no human figure was visible.

Even so, she dared not waste a moment. How long would it take her captors to collect their dole of bread and find sympathetic strangers able and willing to lend them writing materials? Some time, very likely, but she dared not count on it.

She jumped up on the counter, swivelled herself till her legs dangled outside, and launched herself on to the grass. The gorse bushes offered some screen. Her clothes were bone-dry, though crumpled and stained and scented with anything but their normal lavender. She pulled them on. Only her slippers were lacking, lost presumably in the river. But she had often gone barefoot for pleasure and she would not be conspicuous among all these refugees.

She must get away from this spot. Look round for someone respectable, someone in authority. A parish constable, a clergyman perhaps. She had not so much as a penny in her pocket and she was suddenly conscious of her hunger.

She was beginning to get her bearings, though it all looked so different from when she had raced with Boy across the empty grass. Over there ran the long grey line of the ancient city wall, behind it St Paul's with Blackfriars beyond. Now, though, the smoke rising above the ramparts reminded her that she would find only smouldering ruins on the other side. For Shadwell she must turn left and walk round the fringe of the City that the fire had not reached. She would never manage it without food.

People were streaming back to their various shelters, munching hunks of the new-baked loaves that had been distributed. There seemed no shortage. All the bakers in the undamaged area had apparently been busy, at the King's order, producing bread for the fugitives.

Desperate, Sarah was nerving herself to beg when she was spared the necessity. A small boy and his sister were squabbling playfully over a loaf. A piece broke off and rolled away. Sarah pounced. "Have you finished with this?" she asked with gentle sarcasm.

"It's muddy now," said the boy disgustedly and continued the laughing struggle with his sister.

Sarah wiped off the brown smear and sank her teeth into the crust. Never had bread tasted so good. Suddenly the girl was looking up at her, round-eyed. "Would you like this piece too? I've only broken it." Sarah bent and kissed her impulsively. Her lips were rough with crumbs.

She stood, munching blissfully, the fascinated child still staring at her. Then she was aware of a familiar voice muttering behind her.

"It *is* the girl. I told you to *hide* her clothes!"

"We can't do anything now." That was Sukey's wail.

"Can't we?" The man's voice was full of menace. "Look what we've lost in this fire! Here's a chance to get something back. If anyone interferes I'll say she's our runaway servant-girl. Just mind you back me up!"

Sarah stood rooted to the spot. It was as though her heart had stopped. But just then came a diversion – a hollow drumming of hoofs and a delighted outcry, "The King! The King!"

The crowd had been melting away. Now everyone turned and headed for the spot where the horsemen had drawn rein. High in their saddles they stood out, with their huge plumed hats, like a cluster of fantastic flowers.

She picked up her skirts and raced in that direction. Even Gabriel could scarcely drag her away under the eyes of His Majesty.

The crowd had fallen silent. King Charles was speaking. Sarah was too obsessed by her immediate danger to take in much from the phrases resounding over her head.

This was a natural disaster, nobody's fault . . . They should ignore wild rumours of foreign invasions or conspiracies . . . "Every measure is being taken—"

She squirmed her way deeper into the crowd, constantly stealing a glance behind her. In that sea of rapt faces it was impossible to tell if Gabriel was still on her trail. He could do nothing now but he had only to wait his chance. She had seen a runaway apprentice seized by his master in the street and a furious father struggling with a disobedient daughter. The crowd usually sided with the older person. Sukey would naturally support her husband in whatever lies he told.

Ample food supplies, the King was saying, were on their way to London. All churches, chapels and schools were to be thrown open to house the possessions of the refugees. Churchwardens and parish constables would find shelter for those actually homeless, especially the old or sick and the women with child . . .

Sarah edged up to a tall gentleman who, with his fine hat and wig and silver-knobbed cane, looked impressive and influential.

"Your pardon, sir, but this is urgent—"

He bent, looking down his long nose at her with a frown of irritation. "Not now! His Majesty is speaking."

His Majesty went on speaking. "All towns and cities are commanded, without exception, to receive refugees and give them every assistance." Such a catastrophe must never occur again. There would be plans and regulations to prevent future fires. He gave them his word—

The cheering burst out. The cluster of plumed hats broke up like a scattered bouquet. The riders jingled away in a straggling line, the press of people began to disperse. Sarah turned to the gentleman with the silver-knobbed cane but he was already stalking away.

"Got you, my girl!" A hand clamped on her wrist. "D'ye call this gratitude?" She opened her mouth but Gabriel's other hand slapped roughly across her lips. "Young baggage – got to be taught a lesson!" he explained to a bystander. Sukey chimed in to support him. The bystanders backed away uncertainly.

Sarah managed to get her teeth into one finger. She bit, desperately. Gabriel swore. Then he swore again, more loudly and with a new urgency. He removed the bitten hand and she was able to cry, in delighted amazement: *"Boy!"*

The dog was attacking Gabriel, skilfully avoiding his kicks. And Hugh was racing towards her through the thinning crowd.

# 13

Hugh heard Sarah's warning shout: "Take care! He's dangerous!"

The fellow she had been struggling with certainly looked it. But Hugh's blood was up. He could not stop to weigh up the chances of a youth in his teens against this heavily built ruffian. Sarah must be rescued. He rushed on.

The man had landed one kick which had sent the spaniel hurtling backwards. Before Boy could return to the attack the man was away, losing himself in the crowd. And a breathless Sarah, with embracing arms, prevented immediate pursuit. As to that, Hugh felt more secret relief than disappointment.

"*Hugh!*" Sarah had impulsively kissed him. "You *found* me!"

"Thanks to Boy," he admitted. "He must have caught your scent or something. Though how, in all this stinking multitude—" He laughed. "But he suddenly veered off in this direction."

"Clever Boy!" She stooped and hugged the delirious dog.

Questions sprang to his lips but he held them back. Time enough when he had got her safely away from here. She was stammering her own eager questions. Was her grandfather safe? She could not wait to get away from Moorfields.

It was not so far to Shadwell, he reckoned, if one took the straight highway instead of following the curve of the river as he had done. But she could not walk to Shadwell in this state, barefoot, distraught, probably ravenous. Heaven only knew what she had been through.

Food! His own belly was rumbling. Luckily there were enterprising piemen who had crossed the fields from outlying villages and were doing a brisk trade. He bought two pies, their richly seasoned centres warm from the oven. He could see no beer-seller but a milkmaid was passing with pails dangling from her yoke and mugs for the use of customers. Their luck held. As Sarah drained her mug he was able to tell her, "This cart is going to Bow – the man will go round by way of Shadwell if we make it worth his while."

Sarah exclaimed in admiration. "It's nothing," he said airily. "You can arrange most things if you have money in your pocket."

"You seem to have!"

"Mr Bolton said to be prepared for all contingencies."

He wished he had not said that. Fortunately she did not ask him what "contingencies".

Sitting in the back of the cart as it rumbled eastwards they compared notes. He was relieved to find that she had suffered nothing worse at the hands of the man called Gabriel and that his wife, though completely under his thumb, had tried to be kind.

"What a miracle you found me so quickly!" she said.

"I went to Moorfields first because it was nearest. I expect they did too, rather than go out to Hampstead or Highgate at that time of night."

"Well, thank God it's all over now."

The rest of that day was somehow unreal. The ecstatic welcome at Shadwell, Mr Calamy's incredulous joy at seeing Sarah back from the dead, combined with the general relaxation after all they had gone through, left Hugh a little light-headed. Sarah clearly felt the same. By suppertime she was looking exhausted and he too was longing for sleep. But as he stepped outside, wine-flushed, to fill his lungs with the fresh night air, the countryman in him could not fail to observe one thing.

He turned to Sarah. "The wind's dropped!"

She yawned. "What does the weather matter now?"

"It may end the fire."

In the morning there was no doubt of the change. A calm hung over the unruffled river. There was no sign yet of rain. By midday people were bringing more cheerful news from town. Though many buildings were still burning themselves out in various places, and some streets were impassable with smouldering ash, the fire was no longer advancing into the western areas.

Mr Calamy perked up remarkably at the news. He was eager to get back into the City and inspect the extent of the destruction. Above everything, to make sure that the underground dump of books had escaped damage.

Hugh and Sarah exchanged appalled glances. Luckily Mr and Mrs Bolton were there to suggest tactfully that it would be difficult today, if not impossible, and dangerous for a man of his years. He would listen to them, if not to the opinions of the young.

Hugh saw, however, that Grandfather's attitude to him had changed. The old man was almost pitifully grateful for what he had done in finding Sarah. Even before that, though, he had been showing signs of grudging approval. There had been no more talk of Herefordshire. From being an unwelcome guest Hugh had improved his status considerably.

That afternoon they all discussed the future in the Boltons' walled garden in the shade of an ancient mulberry tree.

"You mean to set up in business again?" said the timber-merchant doubtfully.

"Of course. We have to live."

"It will be hard at your age – forgive me—"

The dim old eyes could still flash defiantly. "I am luckier than some. Other booksellers have lost shops, printing presses. I am not tied to Paul's Churchyard. I have Sarah. And it may be . . ." He paused significantly. Hugh was quietly eating ripe mulberries. Mr Calamy's tone caused him to stop, licking the dark red juice from his fingers. "Perhaps this young man – unless he has other plans . . . ?" He eyed Hugh with a questioning look.

Hugh's heart leapt. "I'd be happy, sir."

"We must see how things go."

Mrs Bolton raised another problem. "You will need somewhere to live. If Puddle Wharf has gone—"

Sarah spoke for the first time. "Perhaps Great-uncle William—"

This time the old eyes positively blazed. "Over my dead body!"

"He must have plenty of empty rooms. And the fire has got nowhere near Covent Garden."

"Not a word has passed between us these past five years. I will not go cap in hand to him now. I vowed I would never cross his threshold again. Or let you."

"But, Grandfather, you are brothers!"

"So were Cain and Abel!" Assuming that this retort would flatten her, Mr Calamy turned back to his hostess. "I shall find somewhere. If the Duke's famous fire-break has been effective all Fleet Street should be intact."

Fleet Street! Memories came rushing back to Hugh of the happy days at Mr Jackson's printshop in the quiet courtyard. Suppose Mr Jackson's own premises had stood vacant since his death?

"Well," said Mrs Bolton comfortably, "there'll be a roof over your heads here as long as you need it. All of you." She included Hugh in her friendly smile.

Afterwards, when they were alone, Sarah asked: "Would you like it, Hugh? Working for Grandfather?"

"Nothing better."

"Perhaps—" Her thoughts were racing ahead. "Perhaps the Stationers Company would let him take over the apprenticeship you had with poor Mr Jackson—"

"That would be wonderful." He stifled the realistic thought that Mr Calamy might not live long enough to finish the seven-year period and yet another master might be needed for its completion. One thing at a time. The old man was as tough as leather. If he could solve the other difficulties he might continue to defy old age.

The next morning they found him quite determined to go into the City and see for himself. The other booksellers might be opening up St Faith's and removing their stock. He wanted to be there. Hugh and Sarah could sympathize. The suspense was becoming unbearable.

Normally it would have meant only a leisurely boat-trip to the nearest landing-stairs, but after Sarah's experience no one suggested that. A one-horse hackney coach would carry them quickly along the Ratcliff Highway as far as the Tower. For the last mile to St Paul's they would have to pick their way on foot through the smouldering wilderness. Mr Calamy, keyed up with hopes and fears, was confident that he would be equal to the exertion.

Hugh's dream of Fleet Street faded as soon as they paid off the hackney. A passing seaman told them that the Duke's fire-break along the Fleet had failed in its object. The flames had somehow leapt the barrier. Fleet Street had been destroyed as far as Temple Bar. Only the merciful dropping of the wind had saved the Strand and Covent Garden, and even perhaps the palace of Whitehall beyond.

Hugh thought back to the night he had walked back from Temple Bar with Mr Biddulph. It helped him to realize the scale of the disaster. From the Tower to Temple Bar must be something like a mile and a half. The area devastated must be half a mile wide. The total destruction was beyond imagining.

He had watched Baynards Castle burn, he knew that St Paul's had been gutted. The Guildhall and the Royal Exchange were no more. Other skyline landmarks had vanished or stood up in jagged ruins like rotten teeth. Stationers Hall had gone, apparently, with the tragic loss of all the books stacked inside. Grocers Hall, Fishmongers Hall, and, as he was soon to learn, the halls of forty other City companies. Only weeks later, when all the losses had been reckoned up, would he know that thirteen thousand dwellings had been destroyed and eighty-seven parish churches.

At that very moment, had he but known it, Dr Wren was busy at his drawing-board, preparing a scheme for the reconstruction of London. Within a week or two it would be in the King's hands with half a dozen rival plans. But Hugh would be middle-aged and a grandfather by the time Dr Wren – by then Sir Christopher – was in sight of completing his share of the rebuilding, some fifty of the churches and a completely new cathedral.

That morning, though, as the three of them picked their way gingerly along the straight thoroughfare that had once been Tower Street and Canning Street, it was hard to believe that London could ever rise again.

The smoke hung like a river fog. The cinders underfoot were still fiercely hot, burning the soles of their shoes. The flaky wood-ash, stirred by their feet, glowed briefly red as garnets. In places the drifts of ash were white rather than grey. There were scorched scraps of business letters, bills of lading, pages from ledgers, confirming that here the holocaust had been mainly of paper. Some buildings stood, some were flat with the ground except for an ornate stone doorway or a fireplace and chimney.

Mr Calamy trudged doggedly through the ruins. He had taken the news of Fleet Street remarkably well. At a moment like this his natural obstinacy was an asset. His short-sightedness spared him from the full realization of the damage done. His mood, thought Hugh with grim humour, could be fairly described as blind optimism.

"If the worst comes to the worst," he said cheerfully, "I can hire a cart and take my stock to Westminster. Booksellers can do good business in Westminster Hall."

He did not need much space for his stall. Those already trading there would surely make room for an old and respected member of their company. "Perhaps," he said, struck by a new idea, "I could marry Ann Mitchell." He seemed hurt when Sarah failed to choke back her incredulous laughter.

Ann Mitchell was that remarkable rarity, a woman bookseller. She and her husband, Miles, had long been well-known figures trading beneath the great oak-beamed roof of Westminster Hall. When Miles had died last year of the plague she, as his widow, had been entitled to carry on the business. Hugh had heard Sarah complain bitterly that booksellers' daughters – and granddaughters – were denied that right.

Mr Calamy saw nothing comical in the notion of leading Mrs Mitchell to the altar. He always had a good opinion of himself. His real love was of course the book trade, and he was prepared to make any sacrifice on its behalf.

His eyes might blink in the smoke but they were still bright with the thoughts behind them. He stumped along, Hugh and Sarah watchful that he should not trip. They reached Paul's Churchyard safely.

After all they had seen in the past half-hour they should have been prepared for the sight that greeted them. But Sarah's poignant cry struck Hugh like a blow.

He should have thought. What to him was just one more scene of ruin would be much more to her. Here for the past year she had spent most of her waking hours. Here, usually alone amid a throng of strangers, she had struggled to piece together a life shattered by the loss of her mother. This new disaster must come as a second shattering.

The cathedral itself still stood. Its long roof had fallen in, leaving empty triangles drawn on the sky at either end. The stump of the central tower remained. The gothic windows, their glass melted, paraded their nakedness in a long line. Being largely of stone the church had survived better than the lesser buildings round it.

It was hard to identify some of them – the houses and shops that hemmed the churchyard, the Bell and the White Horse and the other taverns where her grandfather had loved to gossip with his cronies. As for the school, it was a smoke-shrouded heap of rubble. Sarah cried out again. The boys had often teased her and tried to play tricks, but she had stood up to them. They themselves should be safe enough, though some would have lost their homes.

Mr Calamy seemed equally moved. But he was grieving less for boys and buildings than for the High Master's own books. "A schoolhouse can be rebuilt," he wailed. "Latin primers can be reprinted. But Dr Crumlum's own collection – the finest private library in London! He can never have got it away in time."

Some of his bookseller friends had gathered in what had been the choir of the cathedral, directly above their own subterranean church. The floor was heaped with fallen debris, charred roof-beams, shattered lumps of vaulting and

98

other masonry, lead that had melted and set again in curious shapes.

"Perhaps all this may have protected our books down there?" Sarah whispered.

"May well be," Hugh agreed.

The atmosphere was oppressive in that enclosed space. The surviving walls still gave off some of the fierce heat to which they had been exposed. Only freak eddies of hot air disturbed the otherwise windless calm.

Workmen were shovelling away rubble to clear the stone steps leading down to the entrance to St Faith's. Suddenly one of them shouted up the good news that everyone was on tenterhooks to hear. They had moved aside the protecting slabs and the door itself looked intact, the wood not even scorched.

Sarah's grip tightened on Hugh's arm. "Isn't this wonderful? If we can find someone with an empty cart we can get our books down to Mr Bolton's! He'll store them for us until we can start again."

All the booksellers were crying out excitedly, proclaiming their thanks to God. Rivals, who had preferred to store their books in Stationers Hall, had lost them. A similar disaster had overtaken others further east at Greyfriars, where a church had been stacked high with volumes but, not being underground, had been burnt with all its contents. Hugh could not help feeling inwardly amused as he studied the joyful faces around him. Business was going to be good in the months ahead – for those who, like these Paul's Churchyard traders, would still have something to sell. A selfish reaction, but only human. He was glad to think that Mr Calamy was among the lucky ones.

It was quickly agreed that the door should be unsealed, so that those who wished to move out their own stock could start doing so without delay. Joshua Kirton led the way down the steps. John Martin and John Starkey, the Anabaptist, followed. Grandfather was close behind, lowering his weight cautiously from step to step. Sarah and Hugh had to stand back and defer to their elders. They heard Mr Kirton's voice, solemnly calling everyone to witness that the seal had remained unbroken until now. They heard the key turn in the lock, the heavy door squeal back on its hinges, then Mr Kirton's voice again, reporting to the tense listeners above.

"It is very dark inside. Perhaps it would be safe to get a lantern, if we're careful to cover the flame. But my eyes are getting used to it . . . Everything looks just as we left it – it is baking hot of course—"

There was an outburst of pious thanksgiving, mixed with many more worldly – but understandable – reactions.

Mr Kirton's commentary suddenly changed in tone. "Is that a light? A little flame?" he cried almost in panic.

"I smell burning!" Mr Martin shouted.

Then came a sound with which Hugh had become all too familiar in the past few days – an explosive *whoosh!* as a current of air reached some tiny opening bud of fire and fed it. The doorway below was suddenly lit with a leaping brightness. The foremost booksellers became reeling silhouettes, almost blown back into the daylight. Mr Calamy, halfway down the steps, was knocked over. Hugh had to jump down and drag him out of harm's way.

As he did so he caught a glimpse of the crypt's interior. It was like peering into a furnace.

Mr Kirton called, chokingly: *"Shut that door!"*

Someone sprang to obey. Hugh felt an awful certainty that it was too late. The fresh air rushing into the vault when the door opened must have carried some fatal spark from the smouldering ashes outside – and then acted like a gigantic fan. All that paper, slowly dried by the heat from overhead—

Mr Starkey let out a terrible doom-laden cry: "God is not mocked!" He alone seemed to be deriving some perverse satisfaction from the scene. He had argued all along that the fire was the Almighty's punishment for the sins of London. Man's puny efforts to escape would inevitably fail.

Grandfather hardly spoke. "This *is* the end," he managed to say in a tone of utter desolation. Somehow, Hugh scarcely knew how, they managed to get him back, shocked and silent, to Tower Hill. They found a hackney coach in which he sat, apparently dazed, until they reached Shadwell. Only when they had got him upstairs to bed were they free to exchange a private word.

"I don't care *what* he says," announced Sarah with a new determination in her voice. "Tomorrow I am going to call on Wicked Uncle Will."

# 14

Grandfather, Sarah was coming to realize, was a remarkable man.

After that catastrophic morning he had seemed utterly deflated. But when Mrs Bolton had mixed him a potent drink of heated wine, sugar and various spices, he slept for hours and woke asking for supper. It was taken to him in his bed and his vitality came flowing back. Sarah heard him holding forth to Mr Bolton.

"How *can* I give up? I have Sarah to think of."

She ought not to have listened. She should have shut her door or gone down to join Hugh in the garden.

"She is growing up fast," Grandfather went on. "Before we know where we are there will be talk of marriage."

After that, thought Sarah, what girl could be expected to move out of earshot? Grandfather went on – he was apt to go on: "For a suitable marriage she will need a dowry. She is already an orphan, poor girl. And if *I* am to be a pauper . . ."

Mr Bolton tried to get a word in, but kept his voice discreetly low. It was vexing. She would have loved to hear exactly what he was saying. It sounded flattering. He seemed to be suggesting that, with her looks, many young men would be glad to take her without a penny of dowry.

"The young man's parents might think differently," said Grandfather. "She shall have some sort of dowry. I will not have her marrying just anyone. Somehow I will get back into business again."

"But you have lost all your stock!"

"I still have my own books here. I can start by selling them."

Sarah gave a little gasp of horror. Grandfather's own treasured collection had never been for sale though he had been made tempting offers for its rarer volumes. He must never be forced to that sacrifice.

She must seek help from her great-uncle. He could not be the monster Grandfather declared he was. Her childhood recollection was of a kindly, teasing, rather humorous man. The brothers must make up their quarrel. She would bring them together again. That big house in Covent Garden had plenty of empty rooms. Uncle Will would never grudge them a roof over their heads, perhaps even a small loan, until they got on their feet again.

She must not breathe a word of her plan to Grandfather. He would forbid it outright. She must slip away in the morning early, before he appeared. She went down and found Hugh. Would he go with her?

"Of course!" But there was dismay in his voice. "Just when your grandad was beginning to approve of me. He is not going to approve of this!"

"Then I'll go alone!" she said sharply. "If you're afraid of Grandfather!"

"Of *course* I'll go with you! Much worse if you went by yourself. He'd want to send out search parties. I'll go with you – to the death! As the play-actors say." He struck an attitude, declaiming in mock-heroic tones, and her momentary anger dissolved in laughter. "But suppose," he added sensibly, "that Wicked Uncle Will is not in town?"

"I shall leave a letter for him. If Banister and Gibbs still work for him they will remember me. But it's five years ago," she admitted. "There may have been changes."

No need to trouble the Boltons for writing materials. She

went indoors and unpacked her own. Better to write the note tonight, and have it ready if Uncle Will was away. She worded it carefully. If he and Grandfather had been estranged for so long she need not stress the need to be discreet. She begged him to send her a private reply at the Boltons' house.

They set off in good time the next morning. Overhead the sky was clear, the smoke-cloud in front over London now thinning by degrees. They did not take Boy – she could not remember Uncle Will's attitude to dogs and he must not be vexed today.

The first stretch, along the Ratcliff Highway to the Tower, was quickly covered. They chattered almost gaily as they went, full of the new hope her plan had given them. Hugh said he could almost imagine himself on an ordinary walk at home.

"Did you ever walk with a girl?" she asked casually.

He misunderstood. He slowed his stride. "I'm sorry, am I walking too fast for you?"

"Oh, no." She could hardly press her question.

Entering the City they found a change of atmosphere. People no longer stood about bemoaning the ruin. Most were hard at work. Carts rumbled by, lumps of masonry were piled into them, shovels scraped as they cleared the ash and cinders to uncover the flagstones beneath.

In Paul's Churchyard they paused to speak to various people Sarah knew. There were sympathetic enquiries about Grandfather, kind messages to take back to him. The books in St Faith's were apparently still burning and likely to for days. Nothing could save them. Opening the crypt again would only let in a rush of fresh air to fan the blaze.

Not everyone they spoke to was concerned with the book trade and this particular disaster. But all were united in the general misfortune, and united now in a determination to rise above it. Houses could be rebuilt and so could businesses.

The prospect of all this rebuilding had spurred everyone to start clearing his own site. The King wanted London to become a city as fine as those he had seen in Europe when "on his travels", as he tactfully described his years of penniless exile while Oliver Cromwell lived. He wanted spacious squares and long straight streets ending in splendid vistas. Such dreams, however, were already alarming the hard-headed citizens. Land was valuable. Wide straight streets meant that the planners would want to lop off slices and corners of a man's site, when what he wanted to do was to rebuild his property as it had been before, standing on precisely the same ground. It would be safest to get on with the job before the authorities started interfering.

"It will be a fine time for masons and bricklayers," said one man. "It's an ill wind that blows nobody good."

"You might say the same for printers," Hugh murmured. Sarah noticed how he was apt to hark back to his original trade. Like Grandfather and herself he loved books for their contents, but the actual printing of them held a special fascination. The loss of all those volumes at St Faith's, not to mention those destroyed at Stationers Hall and Greyfriars, would keep printers busy for years to come.

They were both eager to get on to Covent Garden. They hurried down Ludgate Hill, staring sadly at the Duke's ill-fated fire-break, and headed along Fleet Street through the blackened wilderness he had failed to save. At Temple Bar they finally left the smoking ruins behind them. The Strand lay before them, unsmirched, splendid in the sun. Beyond it, the clustered turrets of Whitehall Palace, the pale mass of Inigo Jones's banqueting house, the twin towers of Westminster Abbey . . .

They turned right up the gentle slope into Covent

Garden. Sarah could not remember the name of the street where Uncle Will lived. They found the vast central piazza, with its lines of red-brick houses rising on stately pillared arches. It had been used by fugitives from the fire, but only a few of their makeshift shelters remained. Workmen were sweeping up piles of rubbish. The market-stalls she remembered were being set up again along the Earl of Bedford's garden wall.

"Suppose," she said, "we had a stall here and sold books!"

"Why not? Man cannot live by garden stuff alone."

Uncle Will had not lived on the piazza but in a side-street. She would know it when they turned the right corner. They had passed Chatelin's, the fashionable French eating-house which (said Uncle Will) supplied the royal household. Some day, he had promised, when she had grown into an elegant young lady . . . They walked down Russell Street, the Rose – kept, she remembered, by the Long family. When they came to the Fleece, a bigger tavern, she knew they must be near Uncle Will's. It was a favourite haunt of his. When they turned the next corner memories flooded back.

The houses all looked alike, fine though not so fine as those on the piazza. "It was the fifth," she said, counting under her breath.

The house had a closed-up look. Even in this hot September noon not a window was open. Her little "oh" of disappointment turned into an exclamation of horror.

Daubed red across the door were the words, LORD HAVE MERCY ON US, and a cross.

# 15

For Hugh the old plague warning stirred grim memories.

When his first employer had died, those words had been painted across the door, which had then been sealed officially. No member of the household must go out until forty days had passed without anyone else falling sick. Armed guards had watched the house. Sympathetic neighbours had brought food. It had been hoisted up to a bedroom window in a basket and payment lowered with the coins soaking in a mug of vinegar.

The Jacksons had been lucky. They had survived the quarantine without a fresh case developing. Hugh would never forget the intolerable suspense of those weeks.

For Sarah, he now realized, those words on Uncle Will's door must have come as a paralysing blow. He flung his arm round her shoulder, stammering out such words of comfort as came to his lips. With an effort she pulled herself together.

"Oh, *poor* Uncle Will—"

"It may not have been him! I expect he got away to the country."

Likely enough, thought Hugh. Well-to-do people had fled from London. The court had moved to Oxford, the nobility to their various country estates. The mass of the people, with nowhere else to go, had remained at home and often died. Surely a prosperous gentleman like Uncle Will would never have stayed in Covent Garden, where the death rate had been particularly high?

They must sit down somewhere and discuss this new situation. They were both hungry by now. They went back to the tavern where Uncle Will had been a customer. They might get some news of him there.

The Fleece was almost empty. Hugh ordered tankards of small beer, cheap and deliciously cold. They fell eagerly upon the hot meat pasties brought them by a smiling serving wench. Intrigued perhaps by their youthfulness, she lingered at their table and enquired if they had come from the fire-stricken quarter.

Sarah seized her chance. "My great-uncle once brought me here with my mother. Years ago. Mr William Calamy. His house is just round the corner."

The young woman's smile faded. "Poor Mr Calamy! Many's the dozen oysters he's eaten here! A good man, whatever some said. But there, the best are always taken."

"So – he did die?"

"Yes, more's the pity. Didn't you know?"

Sarah explained briefly that contact had been lost in recent years. What with the death of her own mother . . . There was no need to mention the rift between Uncle Will and her grandfather.

"It's been hard for a lot of families," said the woman with quick sympathy. Her own memory of last year was vague on details. So much had happened. "People dying all round you! Too many for proper funerals even, with parsons and mourners and everything." She was hazy about dates. "If you want the date the parish clerk ought by rights to have a record of it." She thought that the poor gentleman had no relatives with him at the time, just his two men-servants.

"Banister and Gibbs! What happened to them?"

"I don't rightly know. They were kept shut up in the house of course, according to the law. But whether they

108

went down with the sickness themselves—" She shook her head. She could not remember everything from those nightmare days. One had lived from hour to hour, never knowing when one's own time would come. "Nobody at the house now, you say?"

"It looked very . . . dead," Hugh told her.

"Well, no one would break in, that's one comfort. Not with *that* still painted on the door."

"Would there be any risk of infection," asked Sarah, "after all this time?"

The woman shrugged. "Some doctors say one thing and some another. And doctors die of the sickness, same as anyone else." A customer walked in and she hurried away to serve him.

Hugh looked at Sarah. "Well – after coming all this way – we could at least knock on the door." She nodded. They emptied their tankards, called good-day, and went.

The house certainly looked lifeless. The small-paned windows stared blankly down at them, grimy with a year of London smoke. No self-respecting servant would have left a door-knocker unpolished for so long. When they used it there was no response.

"Let's go round to the back," she said.

A narrow alley ran behind the houses, which had small yards with pumps and outbuildings. The back door was still sealed and boarded up. No point in knocking. They pressed their faces against the kitchen window and peered inside. Everything looked tidy and in good order, platters and jugs ranged along the shelves, long metal spits in their rack above the fireplace. But there was no fire laid in the iron grate beneath the suspended cooking pot and the line of metal dishcovers were dull with dust.

Hugh's questing eye lit on a casement window that seemed unlatched. With a little coaxing from his knife-blade it swung outwards. He looked at Sarah. "You're a relative. If *you* gave me permission—" He grinned.

She nodded. "I'll come in with you."

"Let me make sure first that everything's—"

It was eerie. He would have been glad of a companion. But not Sarah. Suppose those servants *had* died of the plague. He was nerving himself against the prospect of finding hideously decomposed bodies. He had a sickening memory of helping his father bury some dead sheep. He must spare the girl an even worse experience.

He hoisted himself over the window-ledge, dropped lightly to the flagstoned floor. These were the usual below-stairs quarters opening off the kitchen – a scullery with stone sink and leaden water-pipe, larder, wine-store, everywhere thick with dust. He was startled by a ghostly touch on his cheek – his hand flew up instinctively but encountered only a spider's thread, dangling from the doorway to the steps leading up to the tiled entrance-hall.

The air was musty, hot and dry from a summer's sunshine beating down on long-closed windows. He was alert and fearful for the stench of corruption, but perhaps that would have gone after all these months. Hurriedly he checked each room to make sure that it held no horrific surprises. He crept upstairs. It was indeed a fine house. Dining-room, drawing-room, library – marble fireplaces, wainscotted walls, paintings, and what rows of books! He would have liked to linger there.

This must be Uncle William's bedroom, the great four-poster standing grim and bare as a gallows amid the surrounding splendours. No doubt its hangings and bedding had been destroyed for fear of infection. He climbed more stairs, peering into other bedrooms, heart in mouth. He came to the garrets where the servants would have slept. Here, he thought nervously, if anywhere— But no, the simple beds had been left unmade but there was no sign of the bodies that had once lain in them.

Sarah was calling below. He went down to her, relieved that he had made no sinister discovery. "I got tired of waiting," she grumbled. "I scraped my knee climbing in."

"Was your uncle rich?" he asked.

"He must have been. Or just more clever with money than Grandfather. Lucky at gambling perhaps. Or had useful friends!"

"Or was useful *to* his friends?" Hugh had learnt since coming to London how much corruption there was in high places.

"So many rooms," she said wistfully. "I wonder . . ."

"What?"

"If Grandfather would agree. They were brothers, even though they had quarrelled. Who would say a word now if – just for the time being – I could persuade Grandfather to move in here, until we can find our own place? After all we're 'family', and we've lost our home in the fire, and the King says—"

"It sounds reasonable. Your grandfather's the only stumbling block."

"We must work on him," she said with determination.

The two men-servants, they agreed, must have rebelled against their forty-day quarantine and taken themselves off. That would explain the unlatched window. They had been forced to go secretly and, having broken the law, were not likely to have boasted of it afterwards. There was no evidence that strangers had entered the house to steal.

"Yet there's real treasure here – by our standards," said Hugh. They had gone back into the library to admire the well-stocked shelves. He took out Dugdale's *History of St Paul's Cathedral* with Hollar's splendid engravings. "This would fetch a few guineas."

She let out a giggle suddenly. "And here's the book Uncle Will once snatched from me even before I could open it!"

She held up Pietro Aretino's notorious volume of love sonnets. "Did your uncle read Italian?" Hugh asked.

"He may have done – I don't know. Perhaps he bought it for the pictures!"

"Perhaps he did," said Hugh dryly. They turned over Giulio Romano's decidedly improper illustrations with glee, then guiltily thrust the book back into its place.

"Grandfather could never bring himself to sell anything like that," she declared with a laugh.

"I could," said Hugh frankly, "once I'd got a notion of the price to ask." His business sense had been sharpened when, as a small boy, he had gone with his father to market and listened to the dealers.

Uncle Will's library might be short on theology and devotion, but it was rich in poetry and playbooks – all Chaucer, all Shakespeare, Ben Jonson, and countless other authors. It ranged from French romances to history and travel and scientific speculation. Sarah knew now what her mother had meant when she said, "Uncle Will may have a roving eye but at least he has also an enquiring mind."

They drifted apart, following their own interests along the different bookcases. She came to a recess where Uncle Will's walnut writing cabinet stood. She glanced down at the papers laid out there. Uncle Will was dead. He would not mind her curiosity now. Her exclamation brought Hugh hurrying down the long room.

"Look at this! He was writing his will!"

Hugh looked over her shoulder. It was a brief document, opening with the usual formal phrases. Then the careful handwriting deteriorated, showing signs of haste, the lines slanting across the paper at irregular angles. She had heard that men often put off making a will until some illness warned them to delay no longer. This writing was that of a man suddenly stricken, afraid that he might not have strength to finish his task.

Uncle Will's determination had held out. After listing a few small legacies he had concluded: "*and all else of which I die possessed I give, will, bequeath and devise to my beloved niece Olivia Hazard, whom failing, to her daughter my beloved greatniece Sarah Hazard absolutely.*" The document was signed shakily and dated almost a year before, 20 October, 1665. The servants had added their signatures, *Theophilus Banister* and *Humphrey Gibbs*.

Hugh's voice was husky in her ear. "You see what this means?"

She struggled to keep calm. "I think so." She laughed almost light-headedly. "I can ask Grandfather to come and live in *my* house – as my guest!"

# 16

They could not wait to get back to Grandfather.

They had just enough money between them, after the beer and pasties, to pay their fares down-river to Shadwell – if, that is, Sarah was prepared to get into a boat again. She laughed at his hesitation. "I've made up my mind, I'm not going to be afraid of anything in future. You must hold me to that!"

They left discreetly by the back window, the precious document safe in Hugh's pocket. They cut down across the Strand and plunged into the byways leading to the river. Approaching Popinjay Stairs they heard the cry of a waterman, "Eastward ho!" and ran to catch him before he pushed off.

Sitting side by side in the wherry as it glided smoothly downstream, they could relax and discuss the future. Christopher Wren and his rivals were not the only people that day who were busy with their plans.

"We must get the house fumigated," said Sarah. "Cleaned from top to bottom. Fires in every grate. Herbs, whitewash, tar outside —"

"*I'll* dust the books," he promised slyly.

"And we can weed out plenty we don't want. Enough to set us up in business again."

"You'll have to go to a lawyer first, though —"

"Grandfather will know what to do."

"And Mr Bolton wil advise you. He's so sensible." He was thinking that the merchant was fair-minded and balanced, not swayed by passionate prejudices as Mr Calamy might be.

When they consulted the lawyer, Sarah suggested, Grandfather could also look into the formalities of Hugh's apprenticeship. "If you're still of the same mind," she said.

He smiled. "What do you think?"

"I think we could not possibly manage without you."

"Oh—" He felt he must protest for form's sake.

"I mean it. Grandfather is old. Please God, he will keep his health and strength for some years longer. He has his loyal customers, he knows so much about books – and only he is a member of the Stationers Company. The day-to-day grind will be mine – and yours. He can teach us everything, but until you are out of your apprenticeship we cannot trade without him."

"Of course not." He felt uncomfortable. The obvious thought was in both their minds, would Grandfather live long enough, or would Hugh eventually need a third master to complete the seven-year period.

Sarah changed tack. "I know your heart was in printing originally—"

"Ye-es. But bookselling also—"

"He couldn't continue your training as a printer. But if he could get a licence to print – after all, the Company is for printing as well as bookselling – he could perhaps add a printshop and hire a journeyman to manage it, and you could learn from *him* – I think it would all come within the terms of your apprenticeship. What do you say?"

It was a golden dream. He laughed, trying not to show how tempted he was. He said lightly, "I'd say that you were very clever at planning other people's lives for them."

"What woman has the chance to plan her own? Look at me! A bookseller's granddaughter and competent to run his business. But – it's most unfair – *I* can never belong to the Company."

"Unless—" he began, and stopped.

"Unless?"

"Oh, nothing," he said lamely. What would she think if he said, unless eventually you marry a bookseller? But she could have finished the sentence for herself.

They scarcely noticed when they passed safely under London Bridge.

"And where have you two been?" demanded Grandfather suspiciously when they walked in.

"Covent Garden," said Sarah. And she immediately broke the news of Uncle Will's death. They had already agreed that it would be only seemly to begin with that.

Mr Calamy took it without any display of deep emotion. Uncle Will had been ten years younger than himself. His earlier death must be explained as the wages of sin. "He lived a life of pleasure and now he has paid for it," said Grandfather with grim satisfaction. His main emotion was anger that Sarah had defied his known wishes by going off without permission to call upon him. Hugh sensed that some of this disapproval was levelled at himself for aiding and abetting her.

Sarah flamed red with her own indignation. She cut short her grandfather's tirade by asking Hugh to give her the will, which she then thrust defiantly under the old man's nose. He held it close up to his eyes, piecing out the words aloud, then almost howled, "This is very fine for you!"

For an alarming moment it looked as though he were going to tear the offending document across. He hesitated. Hugh was horrified but dared not lift a finger. Grandfather, however, must have been hampered by his instinctive respect for documents – his sheer inability to destroy anything as important-sounding as this. And while he gibbered

116

incoherently, the invaluable Mr Bolton reached out, gently murmuring, "Will you allow me to look at this?" Without waiting for permission he lifted the paper from Grandfather's dangerous fingers, studied it briefly, and handed it back – not to his old friend but to Sarah. Grandfather recovered his power of speech. "I shall abide by my vow – never will I set foot in that house of ungodliness!"

He refused to discuss the matter further that day. "Your grandfather has naturally had a great shock," Mr Bolton told Sarah. "At his age – I would advise you to let him simmer down. All will be well."

They went to Shadwell church next morning, where the Boltons had their family pew. Grandfather announced, somewhat grudgingly, that he would say a prayer for William's soul. He seemed to imply that his brother would need all the prayers he could get.

Sitting in that pew, the endless sermon rolling over his head, Hugh reflected that it was only a week, almost to the hour, since he had encountered Sarah and Mr Calamy in the church at Blackfriars. Something like a lifetime had been crammed into those seven days. Would everything have changed again when the bells rang out next Sunday?

In the afternoon the discussion of the future was resumed. The old man seemed adamant. He made it clear that these family affairs were none of Hugh's business. Hugh gladly made his escape into the garden, where he played with Boy and ate mulberries.

Suddenly Sarah was beside him. "It's all settled." Triumph twinkled in her eyes.

"You don't mean—?"

"He has mastered his scruples."

"You actually persuaded him?"

"*I* didn't. *I* am 'no more than a child' – *he* thinks." She laughed. "It was dear Mr Bolton."

117

"How?"

"He pointed out that by law the house is mine and it would be unfair to prevent my living in it. But Grandfather is still my guardian and responsible for me. I can't possibly go and live there with only the maids – let alone 'that boy', meaning you!" She stooped and hugged her dog, but smiled up at Hugh wickedly. "Grandfather sees it now as his duty. He admits, on reflection, that it might all work out very well. A proper bookshop, perhaps in the Strand. With space for a printshop at the back – though I haven't mentioned that yet. One thing at a time!"

Tomorrow Mr Bolton would take them to his lawyer. Provided the fire did not flare up again life should soon resume its normal course.

"Even if we have to start with a stall," she promised, "We shall be trading again."

There was a rustle in the branches of the mulberry-tree. More over-ripe fruit plopped softly on to the grass. Instinctively he sucked his forefinger and raised it.

"There's a wind getting up. It's all right," he reassured her, seeing the alarm in her face. "It's moved round to another quarter at last – it's coming from the west. Hold up your finger. There's rain on the wind!"

Already, the first time for many weeks, the big drops would be splashing down on the ruins of Fleet Street. The hot ashes would be hissing their final defiance, the smoke from the smouldering debris would be changing to steam.

Tonight, if the wind held, would see the last of the great fire. Tomorrow a new life would begin.